Pleasure Cruise

▼

I was looking at water. There was hot rain whipping into my face, and a hundred feet or so below me the Atlantic slapped up white-fingered hands to grab me.

I could feel my head going down and my feet coming up, and I didn't really have the strength to fight. So far on this trip, I had survived the Network PR department, the Mafia, the Royal St. David's Island Constabulary, one surly pseudosailor, one homicidal chef, seasickness, one pissed-off dog, one acrobatic librarian, six mystery writers, and a hundred overenthusiastic mystery fans. Added to one decidedly major-league bop on the head, it had all taken a lot out of me. I was on my way into the drink. I roared curses into the hurricane until my throat hurt. It didn't help. The more I struggled, the less my feet gripped the deck.

▲

KILLED IN PARADISE

Also by William L. DeAndrea

Azrael*
Snark*
Cronus*
Killed on the Ice*
Killed with a Passion*
Killed in the Act*
Five O'Clock Lightning
The Lunatic Fringe*
The Hog Murders
Killed in the Ratings

*Published by
THE MYSTERIOUS PRESS

KILLED IN PARADISE

A MATT COBB MYSTERY

William L. DeAndrea

THE MYSTERIOUS PRESS

New York • London • Tokyo • Sweden

MYSTERIOUS PRESS EDITION

Copyright © 1988 by William L. DeAndrea
All rights reserved.

Cover design by Bobbeye Cochran

Mysterious Press books are published in association with
Warner Books, Inc.
666 Fifth Avenue
New York, N.Y. 10103

A Warner Communications Company

Printed in the United States of America

Originally published in hardcover by The Mysterious Press.
First Mysterious Press Paperback Printing: July, 1989

10 9 8 7 6 5 4 3 2 1

This is for Matthew William DeAndrea—
Welcome aboard, kid.

I would like to take this opportunity to thank Bill and Karen Palmer of Bogie's Restaurant and Bogie's Murderous Mystery Tours, Philip DeGrave, Nicola Andrews, and Bob Madison, real people all, for taking time from their busy schedules in order to appear in this book.

1

"Just sit right back and you'll hear a tale,
a tale of a fateful trip . . ."
—The Wellingtons, "Gilligan's Island" (CBS)

I saw stars. Not the heavenly kind, the inside-your-head kind.

I couldn't see much past the dazzle in front of my eyes, but I could hear the champagne bottle, or the rolling pin, or whatever, that had pounded the lights in there as it rolled around the unsteady deck of the S.S. *Caribbean Comet*.

I should have been rolling around on the deck, too, but I've always had a thick skull. And I've always been too stupid to know when to lie down. So I fought the dazzle, fought the pain, fought the near–hurricane force wind and rain that filled my throat every time I tried to open my mouth for a simple breath of air, all in an attempt to keep my feet.

I succeeded, if you want to call staggering like a drunk on a rapidly tilting surface keeping your feet.

The strange thing was, I didn't really care too much about keeping my feet. That was instinct. What I wanted to do was to *see*. There was a three-, possibly a four-time killer on the deck with me, and I think my friend's little love tap to my skull was an attempt to make ace. The M.O. was familiar—the smack to the back of the skull to start things off, followed by all sorts of indignities. I was fighting for my life. I faced the possibility that I might lose (bright little bombs were still going off in my head), but dammit, I wanted to know who was doing it to me.

I rubbed my eyes in an effort to clear my vision, but succeeded only in changing the constellations around a little. The wind blew; the

1

boat tilted. I staggered into a bulkhead. Good, I thought. There are people in there. Miserable, seasick people, but possible help. I started groping around for a hatch.

The *Caribbean Comet* sloshed down the other side of a wave, and the deck fell away from the bulkhead. I started sliding back toward what must be the rail.

This time, I had help. My friend had caught up with me, and was giving me a strong push in the small of the back. I smashed into the rail. The breath *whoosh*ing out of my lungs was lost in the gale. I bent double over the rail, but I held on. The pushing continued. The pushing was winning.

Now my eyes cleared. Thanks a lot, I thought. I was looking at water. There was hot rain whipping into my face, and a hundred feet or so below me the Atlantic slapped up white-fingered hands to grab me.

The way it got Schaeffer, I thought, though I still had no proof of that. But Janski and Burkehart had died, and I was about to join them.

It wasn't that my assailant was using so much strength against me, it was the *leverage*. I could feel my head going down and my feet coming up, and I didn't really have the strength to fight. So far on this trip, I had survived the Network PR department, the Mafia, the Royal St. David's Island Constabulary, one surly pseudosailor, one homicidal chef, seasickness, one pissed-off dog, one acrobatic librarian, six mystery writers, and a hundred overenthusiastic mystery fans. Added to one decidedly major-league bop on the head, it had all taken a lot out of me. I was on my way into the drink. I roared curses into the hurricane until my throat hurt. It didn't help. The more I struggled, the less my feet gripped the deck.

Then a strange thing happened. Another pain forced its way through all the pain that was taking up my attention. It wasn't much, just something digging into my right thigh where it was pressed against the rail. I even knew what it was—a little curved triangle of beige plastic. I'd picked it up a few days ago, and hadn't taken it out of the pants since I'd worn them last.

And suddenly I saw where the piece of plastic fit. I saw where everything fit, and I knew who was trying to kill me. The knowledge made me furious. I *would* get out of this. I had maybe two seconds to figure out how, but I *would*.

It turned out to be less than two seconds. My feet came clear of the deck, and suddenly, I was going over.

2

"Sherman, set the Wayback Machine . . ."
—Bill Scott
"The Bullwinkle Show" (NBC)

Fall is my favorite time of year in New York. The air is as fresh then as it ever gets, and the sky, where you can see it, gets bluer than any sky anywhere. You can walk a couple of blocks in your suit and not be dripping sweat when you arrive. I cherished my early autumns in the city. Now I was going to have to give up a two-week slice of it.

"You're a lucky bastard, Cobb," Marv Bachman told me. Marv was a cheerful-looking, heavyset guy who probably smoked cigars in the shower. Marv was general manager of 102 Dynamite!, which in more sober days had been WTCB-FM, the Network's local FM station. It was our month to lead in the merry-go-round that was New York market radio ratings, so Marv was even more cheerful than usual.

"I'm *glad* he disappeared," Marv said. "Saves me the trouble of firing him. His days were numbered, anyway."

"Does that mean I can call off the search?"

"The search?" Marv looked blank.

"My people have been turning the city over looking for Joe Jenkins. Robert Joseph Janski. You know."

"Yeah, I know the son of a bitch. To my regret. Why?"

"Why what?"

"Cobb, I think you *do* need a vacation. Why are you looking for him? To hell with him."

I took a deep breath, held it for a second, then proceeded calmly. "We are looking for him because that's our job."

It was part of our job, anyway. The sign on my door—white on black, no frills, like everything else around here—says MATT COBB,

VICE PRESIDENT, SPECIAL PROJECTS. My corporate bio says I am the youngest vice president at the Network, but that is only in terms of years. Special Projects tends to age a man. "Special Projects," as defined at the Network, is sort of a Public Un-relations department. When someone at the Network needs to have something found or learned or done, with a reasonable assurance they're not going to read about it in the newspapers, they come to us. Remember that story a while back about the actor who was going to play John Lennon in a TV movie, but got fired because it turned out his real name was the same as that of Lennon's assassin? That was special projects work, or whatever that other network's euphemism happens to be. It was *sloppy* special projects work, since the story got out, but things would have been a lot more embarrassing had the story gotten out after the millions were spent and the movie was in the can.

I didn't point this out to Marv. He knew it. "We are also looking for him," I went on, "because seventeen days ago, when he first failed to turn up for his shift, you called me up and acted as if someone had kidnapped your baby."

"The station is my baby," Marv said, and meant it. "I'd spent a fortune promoting that asshole, and the P.M. drive slot is *important*. You get them in the cars coming home, they've *got* to listen to the commercials."

"That's a reason to keep looking, Marv."

"To *hell* with him, I keep telling you. He was a cokehead, anyway."

"*I* told you that. That he used to be. It's what got him fired in St. Louis. He's been clean for three years. You knew all this when you hired him."

Marv puffed his cigar and smiled. "Yeah, well he must have backslid, right? Or else why did he disappear? To hell with him. Besides, this black guy I got filling in for him is fantastic."

"Marv, Willie Wright has been the weekend man for six years."

"Yeah, but the asshole never told me he was a *minister*."

"He's got a little storefront congregation in Bed-Stuy. Does a lot of good."

"You knew this? *You* could have done me a lot of good and *told* me. Am I the only one with brains around here? Do you hear the crap music we have to play? 'Come into my darkroom of love, oooh, baby

baby, and we'll see what develops'? 'My love is like polio vaccine, it's more fun if you take it by mouth'?"

"Those are not real lyrics."

"No," Marv conceded. "Mostly, what we've got is fake drums and lascivious groans. But it doesn't matter. Because now that it's out that Willie is a minister, he plays the crap, and comes on and explains the Real Holy Lesson in the song. On one station, the listener can get sermons *and* filth. The numbers are dynamite."

"Ah," I said.

"Ah," Marv echoed. "So to hell with Joe goddam Jenkins. He can suck Boraxo up his nose, for all I care."

"Right," I said noncommittally. The Network had a high six-figure contract with Joe Jenkins. The accounting and legal departments would want us to keep looking.

But Marv didn't need to know that, even if he would have listened. Not listening to things you don't want to hear is one of the keys to success in show business, and Marv was a master at it.

"So what's the problem?" I asked. "You could have told me this on the phone."

"The problem is that cockamamie mystery contest you got us into."

My first instinct was denial, but that wouldn't have done any good. I *had* gotten WTCB-FM into it. I have a friend who's a mystery writer, and through him I met a couple of people named Karen and Bill Palmer. They own Bogie's, the chief mystery writers' hangout in New York. Sort of like a specialized Elaine's, only the drinks are cheaper. They also give jujitsu lessons (both hold black belts), host a cable TV show about the martial arts, write books about martial-arts movies, and add to first-rate collections of mysteries, science-fiction books, and films on tape.

In their spare time, they run Bogie's Murderous Mystery Tours, where fans get to go to some interesting place, hobnob with mystery writers, and play detective as they try to unravel an old-fashioned, fair-play murder mystery staged during the course of the weekend, week, or month the event lasts.

The key to running a thing like that, of course, is publicity, and the freer the better. One day, when I was having a drink at Bogie's with my writer friend, Karen said she wished she had access to the Network. I gave her a phone number, and told her to mention my name. She left the bar and went into the office. Ten minutes later, she came back smiling, stood on tiptoe, and gave me a kiss.

It was only a little peck on the cheek but when jujitsu experts' wives go kissing me, the first thing I do is check around for the husband. Billy is about a half a foot shorter than I am, but I've seen him at the heavy bag, and have no desire to fill in for it.

"What was that all about?" I said.

"It's all set," Karen said. "Network publicity said Jim Jenkins was looking for a contest to run on his show—"

"Joe Jenkins," I said.

"Joe? Are you sure?" She always does that. I've often thought she could be the one person in the world who could claim total innocence if she called the wrong name in bed.

"I'm sure."

"Oh, okay. Anyway, we're going to work up a contest, mystery trivia, for a week. We'll get some books autographed to give as prizes for the callers, then we'll have a drawing of the correct callers, and the winner will go on the cruise with us."

"Where to?" I asked idly.

"St. Daniel's Island in the Caribbean. They just got a new administration—"

"St. David's Island."

"Are you sure?"

"There *is* no St. Daniel."

She looked at Billy, who paused in wiping some beer glasses long enough to nod assent. He's Catholic; Karen is Jewish.

"Whatever," Karen went on. "They've just got a new government in, and they and the cruise line want to promote tourism, so we got a deal—"

Billy's dark brown eyes opened wide, and his western-bandit moustache stretched over a grin. "It just sank in. We're getting a week's publicity on the Network's station? On Joe Jenkins's show?"

"I've just been telling you."

He pointed at me. "Kiss him again," he told his wife. "If you don't, I will."

So they had the contest, and everybody had been happy. At least, I *thought* they'd been happy.

"All right," I said, "I got you into it. Me and Jenkins and the publicity department. The contest's over, isn't it?"

"No," Marv said, "the contest isn't over. This Janice Cullen still has to collect her prize, her and her boyfriend or husband or mother or whatever she wants to bring."

"And the cruise starts Saturday, right?"

"Right. But part of the prize was that Jenkins was going to take his vacation, and go along with a tape recorder, and record reactions, how beautiful the Island is and all that crap, and then play them on the show when he gets back. And now he's not here."

"Send another jock," I suggested.

"Such as whom, for instance? I've got my relief man, who is all of a sudden my star attraction, holding down a regular shift. I've got nobody to send until I hire another fill-in."

"Then don't send anybody. I'm sure the contest winner can live without Jenkins as well as you can. The tape stuff would just be more free publicity you'd have to give away."

"That's just the point."

"What's the point? Did you buy into the Palmers' business or something?"

"No, I didn't buy into the Palmers' business or something. I negotiated an advertising and promotional consideration deal with the St. David's Island tourist board that will be worth millions in free junkets to tired Network executives alone. Then there's the money from the ads themselves—"

"How did you do this?"

"They practically begged me to take it. They want to become a major league tourist attraction in a hurry. I think there's a lot of Hong Kong money in this. You know, trying to get as much money out of Hong Kong as they can before the Reds take over."

"So somebody's got to go because you promised postcruise publicity to the *tourist bureau*."

"You got it. And I've got nobody to send."

"You want me to send somebody, then."

He pointed his cigar at the middle of my chest. "I want you to send *you*."

My mind screamed *no, oh God, no—not in the middle of the football season!* My voice remained calm. "I can't just pick up and leave, Marv."

"Sure you can. I already cleared it with everybody."

"For instance?"

"Everybody from Falzet on down." Tom Falzet was President and Chairman of the Board of the Network. I wondered how he knew I liked cool weather and football better than sunburn and seasickness. Falzet's feelings for me were such that he'd never arrange for me to go on a cruise if he thought for a second I might enjoy it.

"I'm beginning to feel sorry for the Islanders," I said. "Against you, they didn't have a chance."

"Davidians," he said. "They like to be called Davidians." I wanted to ask him if he was sure. "My position is this," Marv went on. "If I can't give them a star, I'm going to at least give them a vice president. You can work a tape recorder, can't you?"

When I first came to the Network, I was (briefly) a gopher in local TV news. "I'll puzzle it out," I told him.

"Good," Marv said. "Then it's all set with you, too. Besides, you were asked for. By name. When I talked this over with your friends, they got all excited, how wonderful it would be to have you along on the trip. So I guess you're going."

"I'm going," I sighed. I reflected that my problem was that I had too goddam many friends.

3

"Now let's meet today's contestants."
—Alex Trebek
"Jeopardy" (syndicated)

The prize had been, as prizes in these contests so often are, for "you and a guest." The "you" in this case was Janice Cullen, a former air stewardess who now owned Wooly Thinking, a boutique on Columbus Avenue in the Seventies. For those of you who haven't been to New York recently, or who have gotten your idea of that neighborhood exclusively from *West Side Story*, things have changed. The Upper West Side, especially Columbus Avenue, has become sort of a Greenwich Village for Yuppies. Knowing what commercial rents were like in that neighborhood, I decided one must be able to put away a lot of money on a flight attendant's salary, or that Janice Cullen had been bootlegging airline tickets. Of course, she might merely have been up to her eyeballs in hock to the bank; in which case it was extremely irresponsible for her to take eight days on the bounding main, no matter how many contests she'd won.

The guest was to be Kenni Clayton. *Ms.* Kenni Clayton, as it said on all the paperwork. That was all anybody knew about her, except that she lived at the same address Janice Cullen did.

It was useless to speculate, but that wouldn't stop Marv Bachman. "Probably a pair of goddam dykes," he speculated. "All we need to impress the new goverment, our contest winners get off the boat, they've got shoulders like linebackers, they wear tweed jackets, they've got hair under their arms."

"If they keep the jackets on, no one will notice the hair under their arms."

"Oh, very funny."

"Come off it, Marv," I told him. "These tropical cruise things are like singles' bars that never close. Bringing a boyfriend on one of these things would be like bringing a can of Spam to a butcher shop."

Marv squinted at me over his cigar. "That why you're going alone? Looking to cut off a slice for yourself?"

I ignored him. I have no trouble meeting women—I just happen to meet women who have demanding careers and can't get away for a week in the middle of October on short notice. I'd asked two of them before I got discouraged. I decided it was probably just as well. I'd make more brownie points for the Network if I devoted all my energy to making sure our winners were happy without personal considerations coming in the way. As long as I'd been roped into this, might as well do it right.

On that same theory, I got up a little early the Saturday morning the trip was supposed to start and commandeered a Network's limousine, complete with a driver, to take everybody to the pier. Janice Cullen and Ms. Kenni Clayton lived on West 120th Street, a former hotel remodeled twelve years ago or so to studio apartments. Morningside Heights has never been as bad a neighborhood as some, due to the presence of Columbia University in its midst. There is, however, room for improvement, a lot of which has already been made. Still, I think it's safe to say that this was the nicest car that had parked on that particular block in quite some time that didn't have a crack dealer in it.

The building itself was quite nice, the nicest one on the block. You may have heard the word "gentrification." This is how it works in New York: Somebody puts a nice building in a borderline or outright scummy neighborhood, then charges (this is the key here) a rent that's only slightly silly instead of downright outrageous. Some brave people move in. These can be brave New Yorkers unable to resist a bargain, or new arrivals suffering culture shock over Manhattan rents. Anyway, with luck, most of them live, so the developer fixes up another building, for which he can charge more, since there are now *two* decent buildings, making it a better neighborhood, and so on. By the time the whole block is fixed up, *nobody* can afford to live there, and the process starts all over again somewhere else.

I told Spot to wait in the car while I went and collected our lucky winners. It occurred to me that if these women wore tweed suits, for whatever reason, I'd have to keep Spot well clear of them. Spot is a Samoyed, a breed of medium-sized Siberian sled dog with pointy ears, a cloud of pure white fur, and a perpetual grin on his black lips. Spot was the reason I could keep my interest in the New York apartment market strictly academic. Spot lived in a fabulous condominium on Central Park West, and I was watching both him and it for their true owners, Rick and Jane Sloan, who had spent the last several years doing archeological things in hot, humid places where people were likely to express a savage dislike of Americans at any moment.

If *I* had their money, I'd stay home with the air conditioner on, watch the Discovery Channel on cable, and have all my meals catered, but to each his own. Until they returned, I had the living conditions (and the dog) of the fabulously wealthy.

Anyway, since this was fall, Spot wouldn't be shedding. Too much. For a Samoyed. These things are relative. It would still be a good idea to keep him away from tweed.

I pushed the Cullen button on the intercom. A pleasant voice chirped back. "Who's there?"

"Matt Cobb," I said. "From the Network. All ready to go, Miss Cullen?"

"What? Oh. No."

I smiled. The driver had resented being routed out on a Saturday morning, especially when he found out I had things arranged for us to arrive at the terminal some one hundred minutes before we'd be able to board, maybe three hours before the ship pulled out. I told him I knew women, but that was a lie. What I know is that I *don't* know women. It helps you prepare.

"It's all right, Miss Cullen," I said. "We've got plenty of time, and the car will wait."

"No," the voice said again.

"I assure you it will; the Network owns the car, and I'm a vice president."

"No, no, no."

It was like talking to a two-year-old. Three minutes into this project, and the suave, perfect-host persona was shot.

"I am, too, a vice president, goddammit! One of hundreds, maybe, but I swing enough weight to get a goddam limousine to wait as long as it takes you to get ready. And if you don't want to go on the goddam cruise, it's all the same to me. The Giants are playing tomorrow. And another thing—"

I stopped, because two young women with suitcases were standing behind the glass door, laughing at me. They opened the door. "Hello, Mr. Cobb," the small, dark one said. She had a smoky voice, reminiscent of oiled sandpaper. It was very sexy, but it didn't really go with her dimples or just-short-of-plump curves. She looked like she ought to be bouncy and bright, until you caught sight of her eyes. They were very mature eyes, the eyes of what a friend of mine calls a "Serious Person."

She should have switched voices with the chirper, who was tall and handsome and had a lovely head of hair the color of old bronze. I could not see her eyes, because she was wearing sunglasses. However, since she was also wearing a Hawaiian shirt, shorts over bare (and very nice) legs, and Roman-type sandals, it was a safe deduction she was *not* a Serious Person.

I was a little cheesed off. Looking like a fool frequently does that to me. My self-censor circuits had temporarily shut down. I looked her over and said, "You forgot your beach ball."

She took it in a lot better spirit than I had intended it. She laughed like bubbles and said, "Oh, Mr. Cobb, I'm sorry. I got us tangled all up and diddent know how to get out. We were ready to go . . ."

"Actually, you're ready to *be* there. We've got a couple of days of untropical weather ahead of us yet."

The smaller one smiled wryly. "I've told her that."

"I know it, Jan. I don't mind a little chill." She looked over at the limo. "Although I may be a little underdressed for that car . . ." She shrugged it off and stuck out her hand. "Anyway, the problem is, you were talking to me, but you thought I was Jan. I'm Kenni Clayton, but I couldent figure out how to tell you unless we came down in person."

I took her hand. It was a nice hand. Jan Cullen's hand was a little softer than perfection, but still nice. I said my name a few more times. I called the driver; he and I got the bags stashed in the car—not many, considering we'd be gone a week, and at least twice be expected to dress for dinner—and at last we were under way.

"Spot, stop that," I said. Jan Cullen and I were on the bench; Kenni Clayton had taken one of the jump seats, and absolutely refused my offer to switch. I was just as glad, since I get sick riding backward. Spot was on the floor, rubbing himself against Kenni's long white legs. Maybe he thought they were cold.

"I don't mind," Kenni said. We were all on a first-name basis by now, which was cozy. "He's such a beautiful dog." Everybody says that. "Samoyeds are my favorites. I used to have a dog, but I just couldent keep one cooped up in the apartment all day."

Jan Cullen spoke for the first time since the car got rolling. "You can have a dog in New York if you want to, Kenni. Other people do. The dogs don't mind. Matt obviously does it, and the dog looks fine."

I laughed. "It's his apartment." I told them the tale. "I wonder how he's going to take to a cabin."

Kenni was aghast. "You're bringing him?"

"The Sloans didn't leave me many instructions, but the ones they left they were vehement about. The Arbors is the only kennel in the world, let alone New York, that is good enough for our little Spot, and there were no vacancies, except for one weekend in November, between now and the end of the year. So if the Network wants me on the trip, they get the dog."

Jan Cullen looked at me strangely. I knew what was on her mind, but she was being tactful. Tact, I was beginning to suspect, was not Kenni Clayton's strong suit. She bent over and scratched Spot under his muzzle, a move guaranteed to send him into immediate ecstasy. With her other hand, she raised the sunglasses and looked at me quizzically with very pretty gray eyes. "Why in the world is he called Spot?"

Beside me, Jan Cullen smiled. Now I knew why she hadn't bothered to ask. I suppressed a sigh. That question always comes within five minutes of "what a beautiful dog."

"They named him," I said, "for the gigantic white spot that covers his entire body."

Jan said, "Of course." Kenni said it was cute.

"Kenni," I said, "is an unusual name."

Kenni made a face. "A whole lot better than Mary Kenneth. My mother told my father just before I was born that if I turned out to be another girl, she'd rather raise a daughter named Kenneth than get pregnant a sixth time. So I'm Mary Kenneth Clayton. Yuck. Kenni will do fine."

I barely heard her. I was caught up in the picture of some town somewhere between Baltimore and Philadelphia (judging from her accent) with four more like Kenni in it.

When I tuned back in, Kenni was talking to Jan. ". . . so excited, thanks again for bringing me along, Jan. I don't know when I'd ever get the chance to do this on my own."

"Don't be silly," Jan said. "I'd probably have asked you to come along, anyway, but considering you won the contest for me, I couldn't very well have left you home."

Kenni smiled impishly. "No, I guess you couldent." These are not typographical errors, by the way—diddent, couldent, wouldent—this is the way she talked, as if all her contractions were brands of toothpaste.

Jan turned to me. "I was destined to go back to St. David's Island," she said.

"Back?"

She nodded. "When I was flying, the old regime there tried to promote tourism. They talked Columbia Airways into running a couple of flights a week there. I filled in once. It didn't work out."

"What was wrong?"

"They didn't realize you need more than beaches and weather to make a resort. Like hotels and restaurants and things to do at night."

"They're supposed to have rectified that."

"So I understand," she said. "Anyway, it was such a bizarre combination of circumstances that led to my winning this contest. I had *just* hung up the phone after a wrong number, or my line would have been busy and they would have called somebody else. Kenni just *happened* to be there, dropped in for a cup of coffee, when the phone rang and that disk jockey—what's his name?"

"Joe Jenkins."

"When Joe Jenkins called—"

Kenni broke in. "Is his disappearance part of the mystery? On the ship? That we're supposed to solve?"

I told her I didn't think so.

Jan laughed. "You see what I mean. I *just* manage to get the phone call, and I *just* happen to have a mystery nut dropping in, so when Jenkins asked me the bank some character worked for—"

"John Putnam Thatcher, by Emma Lathen," Kenni said, authoritatively. "The Sloan Guaranty Trust."

"—we were on our way to the Islands."

Spot now had his head on Kenni's knee. A mystery expert, eh? "What if he'd asked you who Emma Lathen really is?"

"Mary Jane Latsis and Martha Henissart."

"You're not going to get her that way," Jan said. "Kenni is in charge of the children's room at one of the branch libraries. And unofficial mystery buyer for the whole New York Library System. She reads this stuff for a living."

I smiled at her. "Nice work, if you can get it."

"There's the terminal," Jan said.

Kenni wiggled. It's hard for a tall woman to wiggle with joy gracefully. but Kenni managed it. "I'm so excited. Yes, it's a fine job, and I love it, but it gets to be awfully routine. That's why I've gone native so soon. I'm sick of wearing a damned *tweed suit* all the time."

I couldn't even tell her what I was smiling about.

4

We were VIPs. It said so right on the little envelope next to the fruit basket, under the bottle of champagne on the dresser in my cabin. It was an invitation from Captain Lars Gustafson, to a Captain's Reception in the Starview Lounge on the bridge deck. Dress was informal, which, I reflected, was good news for Kenni. I toned myself down to a sports jacket, turtleneck, and clean jeans. If the captain didn't like it, I'd come back to the cabin here and take a nap.

There were a couple of things I wanted to do before I went upstairs. Excuse me. "Above." There are two kinds of people—those who can pick up nautical terminology and those who can't. I can, but the minute I hit land again, I forget it all. At various points of our tale here, I'm just as likely to say bathroom for head and stairs for ladder and floor for deck as not. Forgive it please. Also forgive the lack of detailed statistics about the ship (not boat). They're not important. All you have to know is that there were five decks and a bilge, the ship drew about twenty feet of water, and it was going to go about thirty-five knots, weather and current permitting, all the way to St. David's Island.

The crew was as stratified as British society of the nineteenth century.

Captain Gustafson and all the officers were Norwegian. The ship, though American owned, was Norwegian registered. The ship's engineer was a Scot. I found out that all ship's engineers in the Free World are Scots. It's like a rule. The actual crew, the people who worked hard and sweated, and whom we never saw, were Filipinos. The cabin stewards were Koreans. Everybody else who dealt with the

17

passengers (the Cruise Staff, the literature called them) were Americans, except for the people in the kitchen and the dining room, who were Davidians, and the ship's surgeon, who was Japanese, and don't ask me how he got there. Don't worry about any of these people except for the captain, Dr. Sato, and a few others, whom we will get to in time.

Where was I? Right. Two things I wanted to take care of before I collected our winners and went above. First I read the rest of the literature—"Welcome to the S.S. *Caribbean Comet*," containing all the information I just gave you and lots more; "If You Bring Your Pet," containing rules which I considered reasonable for keeping a dog with you on the trip, and please, won't you let us make him comfortable in the hold?; and the ship's newspaper, which reported events on the ship on one side of a mimeographed sheet, and nodded toward the happenings in the Outside World on the other. There was no mention of Tropical Storm Iris, now brewing in the direction we were heading, but what the hell. The ship held a thousand passengers; it was bringing about seven hundred this trip. At least a hundred of those, Billy and Karen's mystery fans, could read, and everybody had access to a radio or TV set. If we were assholes enough to take off across the ocean in the middle of the hurricane season, served us right.

The other thing I wanted to do was introduce Spot to the cabin steward. The rules in the brochure didn't say we'd appreciate it if you could keep your attack-trained pet from reducing our cabin staff to a pile of bloody hunks, but you can't think of everything.

There were two bunks in my cabin, which struck me as a little strange, since even if I had been able to get a date I doubt we would have used two bunks, and each one had a little button near it. I pushed it, hoping it wasn't a fire alarm or something.

He was knocking on the door almost before my finger left the button, and I had a vision of the winter provisions of an entire village in Korea depending on the size of the tip I gave Kim.

That was his name, he said. When I told him that would have been my first guess, his smile changed from the pasted-on one of eager subservience to one that took me in as a human being. I appreciated it.

I introduced Kim to Spot and vice versa. I told Spot Kim was his friend. Spot would have to take my word for it. Smile A was back on

Kim's face. He said, moving his lips as little as possible, "Russian dog." I got the impression he did not like Russians.

"A defector," I assured him. "Generations ago. True-blue American."

Kim shrugged and left it at that. Then he said something that was undoubtedly the Korean for "What a beautiful dog," and scratched Spot behind the ear. Then he smiled, bowed, and left.

He didn't know it, but he had raised his tip twenty percent. He was the first person ever not to ask me why he was called Spot.

The Starview Lounge was built above the bow of the ship, with big windows all around. Right now, of course, the only star in view was the sun, and the air conditioners were striving mightily to counteract the greenhouse effect. I was eating Pepperidge Farm Goldfish crackers and drinking club soda with lime, six ounces a shot. I can hold six ounces of club soda in my mouth, but I had given up trying to get bigger glasses, and was ordering them two at a time. Jan Cullen was · sitting beside me, drinking Campari and soda. Kenni was mingling. I stayed with Jan because, no matter who knew where John Putnam Thatcher worked, Jan was the official contest winner, and Kenni needed no help in mingling.

"She's amazing, isn't she?" Jan didn't seem to think the question needed an answer. "Who's that she's talking to now?" She made an unobtrusive gesture with her glass in the direction of a large, heavy guy with black-and-white hair and a beard to match.

"Oh, that's my writer friend. Philip DeGrave. He's the one who introduced me to the Palmers and some of the other writers on this trip.

"Philip *DeGrave*?"

"A woman named Kenni should get along with him just fine. He named his son Doug, I guess to prove he has a sense of humor. That's his wife next to him. She's a writer, too. Nicola Andrews."

Jan looked mildly surprised. "Oh. I've heard of her."

"Sure," I said. I took a sip of club soda. "I figure if your best friend is a librarian, you've got to read something just to be polite."

"Wit," Jan remarked, just to show she recognized it when she heard it. "What I meànt was, she wrote that book about the airline stewardess who takes over the plane and crashes it into St. Patrick's Cathedral. Was that a mystery story?"

"Don't get DeGrave started on that one. His theory is that publishers believe a book ceases to be a mystery story after it sells a certain number of copies. Or maybe you should get him started—he can be fun to watch. And he's persuasive, too. The first time I heard his spiel, I got wildly indignant over something I didn't give a damn about."

A lot of people were smoking, and the lounge was rapidly becoming a little bit of Los Angeles. Jan peered through the haze. "They appear to be hitting it off. The woman is giving Kenni her address or something."

"Kenni is writing a mystery story," I suggested. "Nicola adopts unpublished writers the way some people adopt puppies. She's given a lot of people their first break."

Jan rolled her eyes. It was the biggest reaction I'd seen from her yet. "Oh, God, Kenni's written four of them, and that's only in the three years I've known her."

"Rejections? Nicola has rejection stories. I bet every writer in the place except for Schaeffer has rejection stories."

Jan gave me a look. "Schaeffer? Lee H. Schaeffer? I've heard of him, too."

"Of course you have." Lee H. Schaeffer was the current Big Thing in Mystery. They come along every few years. You can tell, because either *Time* or *Newsweek* does a big article about how they've reinvented the mystery story. This (according to DeGrave, who has a veritable menagerie of pet peeves) proves two things—that just being a mystery writer is not intellectual enough for guys who write for newsmagazines, and that guys who write for newsmagazines don't know much about mystery stories.

Anyway, Schaeffer was an especially big Big Thing. He'd made the *cover*. He wrote a series of books about a private eye named Stephen Shears, who lived in Aspen, Colorado, was a Nordic skiing and marathon fanatic, made his own beer, bread, and cheese, and thought deep, half-tough, half-sensitive thoughts about the Meaning of It All. Especially the Emptiness of Money, and his Code of Manly Ethics.

I hadn't met Schaeffer yet, but there was a week ahead of us. Kenni, it seemed, would be able to introduce us, since Schaeffer had horned in and was resting a meaty hand on Kenni's arm as he carefully edged his broad back in front of Phil and Nicola. Phil was going to say something, then thought better of it, probably because of an elbow in the ribs delivered by his wife. I caught his eye, and they came over to join us.

"Congratulations," Phil said. He sat down heavily and asked me how the club soda was. He doesn't drink. I do, but not before sundown.

"We were talking to your friend," Nicola said to Jan. "What does she expect to find on St. David's Island, gold?" Nicola has been everywhere—Cambodia, just before it fell, Afghanistan, just before it fell. She's been investigated by the State Department, but it's merely a thirst for adventure, not subversion. Phil has managed to slow her down a little. It occurred to me that I ought to introduce her to the Sloans.

"What do you mean?" Jan asked.

"She's so excited," Nicola said.

Jan smiled that slow smile again. "I think it's meeting you people, really. She's the mystery fan around here. She reads all your books for the library, and she writes her own, but won't let anybody read them—"

"Nicola will fix that," Phil said around a mouthful of Goldfish.

"We're just writers," Nicola said.

"Who bruised her jaw on the table when she met Stephen King?" Phil asked.

Nicola made a face. "That was different. I mean, *Stephen King.*"

"And I keep telling you. You're *Nicola Andrews*. If the italics aren't there yet, they will be soon. The only thing that can keep it from happening is excess modesty on your part. Now you change the subject."

Nicola patted his hand. "Yes, dear." She turned to Jan. "What do you do, Miss Cullen?"

They started talking about woolen goods. Phil got tired of waiting for a tray, and volunteered to take a run up to the bar. I waved to people. Mike Ryerson, a big, rumpled bear of a guy, had written an even fifty novels as we set sail, under five different names, one of them his own. His talk (according to more of the literature I had read in the cabin) was going to be on the topic "Five Writers for the Price of One." He was talking to Althea Nell Furst, author of best-selling romantic suspense, a woman who could give lessons in how to look like a librarian if Kenni ever happened to need any. Even now, she was wearing a tweed suit.

Kenni had changed from the beachcomber outfit before we'd come up here, but she still didn't look like a librarian. She was wearing a shirtwaist in dark blue silk, a string of pearls and pearl earrings, and looked, not to put too fine a point on it, great. Lee H. Schaeffer had closed the distance on her. He was tall and bony—broad—not especially muscular, but not likely to be mistaken for a concentration camp survivor the way some runners are. When he turned his head, I could see Kenni's eyes dart back and forth, as if looking for help. I sighed, offered excuses to Nicola and Jan, who were talking about something called merino, and couldn't care less if I left, and headed over.

Billy and Karen bustled into the lounge carrying a ton of papers just as I passed by the exit.

Billy said, "Matthew!" and Karen asked me how things were going.

"Nice party," I said. "How's it going on your end?"

Karen rolled her eyes. "Half our contestants signed up for first seating! Including your contest winner! All the group meetings are during the first seating! I *told* the cruise line not to let any of our people sign up for first seating. I've got it in *writing*!" She started unzipping a leather folder.

I put out a hand to stop her. "I believe you, Karen."

"Oh," she said. "Of course."

"I was just heading over there." I pointed at about waist level in the right direction. "Your big guest star is coming on a little strong to one of the Network's contest winners."

"Oh, the contest winner. The tall blonde. Janice Cullen?"

"Ms. Kenni Clayton," I said. "Actually the guest, but still."

"Can't say as I blame him." Billy made a Groucho Marx face, something he's very good at.

"Very funny I'm sure," Karen said. "I was afraid something like this would happen."

"What do you mean?"

"Mindy left him."

"Mindy? The one he dedicates all his books to? 'The wind at my back, the sun in my eyes, the flame in my heart'? That Mindy?"

"Don't make jokes," Karen said. "This is serious." I figured it must be serious. She got the name right and everything. "It happened the other night at the restaurant. She called him a conceited old fart and walked out on him."

I looked at Schaeffer. He couldn't have been much more than forty-five. "He's not that old."

"Compared to Mindy he is," Billy said. "She was a student in his writing course when they took up with each other. A sophomore. What was it, five years ago?"

"Ah," I said. I had forgotten that before he became the Big Thing, Schaeffer had been a professor of American Literature at NYU. A de facto Greenwich Village intellectual. A certain type of coed considers her education incomplete until she's had an affair with one of these guys. You meet them in New York all the time; they'd just as soon tell you about their youthful indiscretions as not. Usually they roll their eyes and say, oh, God.

Mindy had lasted about twenty times longer than most, but had in the end walked out just like the rest of them.

"So Schaeffer's like a man who just fell off a horse."

Karen made a face. "He's what?"

"Can't wait to get back in the saddle," Billy explained.

"Only this filly don't look like she wants to be broke. Look, go tell Schaeffer you've got some books you need him to autograph, and I'll see to my charge."

We went over. It was a more complicated operation than I'd hoped—Schaeffer was boring in for the kill, and wasn't about to be distracted by mere autograph seekers. Kenni was starting to panic.

"Excuse me for interrupting," I said suavely. "Kenni, Network publicity has a man here; they want to get some pictures of you and Jan on deck before the ship sails. It's getting close, and I don't want to haul a photographer all the way to the Carribbean, so if you'll just come with me . . . ?"

"I'd think you'd want some pictures of these lovely young ladies with the celebrities. Shall we go?"

I looked at him. It's okay to be a celebrity. It's even okay to think of yourself as one. It is a mistake to announce it in tones utterly devoid of irony. It makes you look—well, it makes you look like a conceited old fart.

I smiled at him. "We've got a whole layout planned for the

Island," I said. "Palm trees, celebrities, contest winners, mystery under the sun, like that."

Marvelous, I thought, now I'll have to spend thirty bucks of the Network's money to send a cablegram back to Marv Bachman and get him to set this up.

"Well, I'd like to take a stroll on deck, myself."

Billy came to the rescue. "Gee, I'm sorry. Karen is just about to introduce you to the crowd." The fact that the crowd consisted exclusively (at this point) of "celebrities," people here to see them off, and officials of the cruise line, all of whom presumably knew who everybody else was, momentarily escaped him. I don't think it's a good idea for people to leave New York and move to Colorado. Brains used to working on dust and exhaust fumes have a tough time adjusting to thin mountain air.

Then Billy made a mistake. He introduced us formally, adding, "You and Matt can have a long talk later. He's solved some real-life murders."

Schaeffer's eyes narrowed. "Oh, really."

"Not really," I began, but Billy cut me off.

"He's being modest. The Lenny Green murder—Matt figured that out. And there was one upstate—"

Schaeffer's habitually bluff tone became positively deadly. I think it would probably be safe to say that by now, he hated my guts. Not only was I about to snatch a lovely young woman away from him, I was a man (as far as he could see) who took the macho trips in reality he had become a "celebrity" only fantasizing.

I thought of shrugging it off, of saying I got into these things by an accident of my job, I hated it when it happened, and only saw them through with a combination of panic and good luck. This would have the virtue of being the absolute truth, but somehow, I didn't think Schaeffer would see it that way. He'd see it as the kind of phony-humble macho bullshit posturing he would have done, and he'd hate me worse for it.

I shrugged apologetically. "That photographer really is going to have to swim back, if we don't hurry." I gestured Kenni toward the exit. I didn't want to touch her. Men touch women, uninvited, altogether too much, and I was supposed to be rescuing Kenni from that.

When we got out on deck, Kenni let out a big sigh. It was hot, but we were away from the cigarette smoke. It was fun to breathe again.

"Where's Jan?" Kenni asked.

"Billy will send her out to us in a second. I hope he will. If only to make it look good."

"Make what look good?"

"There's no photographer."

"I don't get it."

"It was the only way I could think of to get you out of there without pissing off the Palmers' main drawing card. You *looked* like you wanted to get out of there. If I read the signals wrong, no harm done. You can go back in. I'm sure he'll be glad to see you."

Kenni hooted with laughter. "I couldent have stood another minute. I would have slapped him minutes ago, but he's so *strong*. He was grabbing my arm through my sleeve all the time he was telling me how he was going to make mystery stories into real literature. I wouldent be surprised if he gave me a bruise."

"He's a desperate man." I told her about Mindy.

"You men really stick together, don't you?"

"What do you mean?"

"Making excuses for him." She pouted. "I really like his books, too."

"There's a difference between an explanation and an excuse." I looked at her. "Look, lots of people take these cruises to get lucky. I don't care if Schaeffer does or not. He probably will, there are probably enough mystery groupies on this ship to make him forget Mindy, at least for a week. But my job is to see that you and Jan have a good time. You can get lucky, too."

She threw her head back, and the wind blew her hair, and pressed the blue silk against her, and she tried to be haughty. "Thank you very much for your kind permission, Mr. Cobb." The effect was somewhat spoiled by the fact that she was blushing red as a box of Valentine candy.

I was exasperated. "My only point is, it's up to you. It's not up to Schaeffer or anybody else. I'm sorry if I—"

The ship's whistle gave a warning blast. Ten minutes. The deck started to crowd with people who wanted to see the dock recede. Kenni smiled and mouthed (though she could have been screaming it, for all I could hear), "It's okay."

The whistle died away. "Here's Jan," I said, pointing through the crowd.

Kenni didn't follow my finger. Instead, she looked up at me (not too far; she was a tall woman) and said, "*I* diddent know you solved real-life murders."

5

One thing I hadn't reckoned on when I brought Spot on this trip was the inadequacy of the ship's newspapers for canine sanitation. I discussed the problem with Kim, and he brought me a supply of plastic sheets from the ship's laundry. They were thick and strong, a lot better than the ones you get from land laundries. I brought a sheet and the dog on deck, he made use of them (although there are damned few acceptable things on the deck of a ship for a dog to pee on), and I threw the stuff over the side, expecting that a Coast Guard cutter would come along at any second and haul me off to jail for polluting the Hudson River, which we had not yet left. A loyal New Yorker to the end, however, I had made sure to throw it off the Jersey side.

I walked Spot around for a while, then I went back to my cabin. I had to smile as I put the key in the lock. Just after the captain's party broke up, Karen came up to me and apologized for my cabin location.

"Why?" I asked. "It's above the waterline. It's got a bathroom. A head, I mean. The steward and I get along fine."

"Well, we've got the writers and Billy and me up on A deck. We would have put you there, too, but we couldn't get a cabin for your contest winners, and we figured you'd want to be close to them, so we put you down on C deck. That's where most of our people are. They're really perfectly nice accommodations."

"I just said that."

"What?"

"Never mind. You mean I could have had a cabin on A deck? Right under the disco floor? So I could hear loud thumping rock music and screams of drunken revelry all through the night? I'm crushed."

"A deck is right under the disco floor?" She looked slightly sick.

"Check out the plan of the ship they gave you. That's how it looks to me."

"Oh, God. I'd better do something about this."

"Such as what? Your paying customers will sleep better, if sleeping is what they want to do. The freeloaders have to stick toilet paper in their ears. Sounds fair to me."

"You're a free—you're our guest, too."

"I got lucky for once. Also, I'm traveling with a very sensitive dog."

She looked at her watch. "I can't even worry about this, now. The organizational meeting is set for five o'clock."

My contestants had gone exploring the ship's shops. They would soon be able to explore the stores of an entire country, but God forbid they should miss an opportunity to see a store window on shipboard.

I let myself into my cabin. Spot lay down on the rug and went to sleep. It sounded like a good idea to me, but before reforming from my life of crime, I wanted to do one more forbidden thing—I went to the porthole, unscrewed all the stays, and opened the thing up. They didn't want you to do that because it wasted air-conditioning. I am probably America's foremost fan of air-conditioning, but I like the occasional bit of fresh air, too. I didn't intend to abuse the privilege, but it was nice to know I could get some if I really needed it. Besides, I wasn't ever about to open the thing all the way. Spot could fit through the hole on one jump and muss nothing but his fur. I could see it now. "But Matt, where's my *doggie*?" "Sorry, Jane, lost at sea. We held a service." No thanks.

I screwed the window shut again, decided not to wipe my fingerprints off it, stripped down to my underwear, and lay down on the bunk away from the sunlight.

I *think* my upper and lower eyelids touched before the alarm went off. To say it was a bell was to say Dolly Parton is a girl. This was a loud, insistent, merciless, and unending din. I jumped up screaming (though I couldn't hear myself) and saw Spot on the other bunk, trying to dig a hole in the mattress to hide in.

Eventually, the bell stopped, and my brain could start working again. This was undoubtedly the mandatory boat drill. It didn't have to be that mandatory. All they'd have to do would be threaten to ring that goddam bell again, and I'd do anything they wanted.

I made my way up several flights of ladder (or however the hell they say it on a ship) to the boat deck, which on this particular vessel was above A deck. I met Jan and Kenni on the way. Kenni was carrying a small bag with the ship's logo on it.

"How do we find it?" Kenni asked.

"Just go where you hear the person calling the range of numbers that includes your cabin."

We did. We wound up standing in front of boat Number 21, which was my old basketball number, and seemed somehow comforting. We stood there for ten minutes, holding life jackets under a Plexiglas-covered arcade, the greenhouse effect of which made the Starlight Room look like an igloo. People were still straggling in. "How long does it take a ship to sink, anyway?" I wondered, and a stewardess rewarded me with the dirtiest look I have ever gotten from a woman whose name I didn't know.

Some people were showing what old hands they were by grousing about having to go through this again. Some people were treating it like a lark. After opening my mouth once, I decided to take it all stoically.

Then Kenni, standing beside me, gasped.

"What's the matter?" I asked.

"Where's Spot?"

"He goes down with the ship," I said.

"You wouldent!" She was serious.

"Of course not," I assured her. "He gets my place. I just put the Mae West on him, then *I* go down with the ship. Once his owners got hold of me, I might as well have, anyway."

"Matt, this izzent funny! You're responsible for that dog."

"Well, if we get in trouble, you can talk one of these nice people into giving up his seat for a dog. Good luck."

The stewardess started to read off names and cabin numbers. Jan turned to me and whispered. "I know one person I wouldn't mind seeing miss the boat." She pointed discreetly back over her shoulder.

I looked, but I heard him before I saw him. In our little bunch for boat Number 21, Lee H. Schaeffer, holding forth in a stage whisper to the effect that this was all a waste of time. Very few people had the guts to take proper action in a crisis. In an emergency, all would be panic and chaos, and those who couldn't keep their wits about them would drown like rats.

Kenni shuddered. "Spot can have my seat. I wouldent *get* on a life raft with him."

"Yeah, but what a writer. 'Drown like rats.' I wonder where that came from? Did you ever try to drown a rat? I have seen a social-climbing rat swim clear across the Hudson from New Jersey, climb up on a dock, pull over a garbage can, and begin to eat."

"Do you think there are rats on this ship? Four-footed ones, I mean." Jan looked apprehensive as she asked, damn near scared. So I said no. Actually, there probably were some I read somewhere that every vessel above a certain size is bound to have rats. But I'm a New Yorker. If they stay away from the room I'm in, that's all I ask

Finally they stopped calling names, they showed us how to jump into the water without breaking our necks on the life jackets, and they let us go I checked my watch and saw I could still get something like a decent nap before the mystery cruise briefing, and offered to carry Jan and Kenni's purchases back to their cabin.

Schaeffer caught up with us before I reached the stairs. Ladder

"Cobb!"

"Yes, Schaeffer?" He squinted at me, perturbed for a second. I think he expected me to call him Mister.

"I've been asking around about you."

"Whatever for? I'm no celebrity."

"People who get involved in murders interest me "

"It isn't fun. I much prefer mystery novels."

"No, I don't suppose it would be, when your best friend is arrested in a messy sex scandal."

I looked at him. He really was a remarkable phenomenon. He was taller than I was, and absolutely rectangular. He had a long neck, but no discernible waist. With his shock of carefully blow-dried, black hair, he looked as if someone had stuck a wig on a folded lawn chair. There wasn't much to see in the way of muscle, but the muscle was there. I could feel the strength in him when he'd clapped me on the shoulder to get my attention.

He was leaning toward me, now. Not exactly leaning—it's hard to lean without a waist. It was as if he were hinged in the middle, like a garage door, and the top half had slid toward me He had an okay face. His eyes were intelligent and fierce. I was beginning to dislike him as much as he disliked me.

"No," I said quietly. "It was a drag."

"Or one of your employees turns out to be a triple murderer."

"One of my subordinates. He was the Network's employee. As a writer, you should be more careful with words." I suppressed a grin as I saw him flinch. I went on before he could say anything.

"But no, that was no fun, either. I can only think of five times in my life, including right now, when I've had less fun. Do you have a point, or are you just trying to ruin my trip?"

People were coming up. Schaeffer lost the glare and gave me the smile of good fellowship. "No such thing. I'm trying to add a little excitement."

"If I wanted excitement, I would have stayed in New York and watched a football game."

"That's the other thing I found out about you. You're quite an athlete."

"I played basketball in college. Wednesday nights when I'm free, I play volleyball at a grade school gym on the West Side. Why?"

Schaeffer looked sly. "I thought we might engage in a little friendly competition."

"I don't think so," I said. I was beginning to doubt Schaeffer and I could engage in a little friendly anything.

"A round of golf when we get to the Island?" he asked.

"Never played the game," I told him.

He clicked his tongue. "And you an executive."

"I could never see the point of walking after a stationary ball, hitting it into a stationary hole, then telling yourself you're an athlete."

"Tennis, then."

"You know all these rich man's games, Schaeffer."

We were being childish, and I knew it. Doesn't mean I could stop. Males strutting in front of females was bred into us when it made a difference to the survival of the species that the ones with the most muscles got to reproduce. I suspect it's going to take rationality a million years or so to catch up with evolution.

Kenni would have made a good Cro-Magnon woman. She had latched onto my arm and was looking daggers at the interloper. Jan, on the other hand, seemed to know how big a couple of assholes we were being—she had her back turned to us, studying rivets in the bulkhead like an apprentice boat builder.

"Come on, Cobb," he said. "I'm almost half again your age. You can't be afraid of me."

And like a jerk, I let it sting me. I didn't want to have anything to do with this business, but I absolutely was not going to leave the slightest idea in Jan's or Kenni's mind that I was afraid of him, either.

"They've got a gym on this ship, right?"

"Yes, they do."

"What's in it?"

"A Nautilus." He grinned. "You want to lift? Against me?"

"You want to go one-on-one hoops against me?" He didn't answer. I went on. "Are they set up for table tennis?"

"*Table* tennis?"

"Ping," I said. "Pong. You know."

"Ho. They have one. You're going to wish we lifted. As soon as we get to port."

I shook my head. "Uh-uh. Tonight. The sea is flat as glass, and you're going to make my life a goddam misery until we get this over with. Right after Billy and Karen's little mystery game."

"Ten o'clock, then."

"Ten o'clock it is. Ladies, shall we go?"

"Just a minute, Cobb."

"Now what?"

"How about a little wager."

I turned to him and smiled. "Sure, I said. What did you have in mind?"

"A hundred dollars?"

"A hundred dollars? But Schaeffer, you've had six best-sellers and three hit movies, plus a TV show. You must be a millionaire. A hundred dollars must be nothing to you."

"I didn't want to make it too rich for you."

"I quote a well-known fictional detective: 'The worst thing about money is that it makes people who have it think they're worth something.'"

"That's mine. You have better taste than I thought."

"I never said you couldn't write. I just think you're full of it. But that's beside the point. There are things other than money to bet."

"Name it."

"Loser gets up in front of the Bogie's group at the earliest possible opportunity, announces the result of the game, and declares himself to be an asshole."

"You sure you want to admit that to everybody?"

"If I lose, I'll do it. How about you?"

He stuck out his hand and we shook on it. He tried to give me a crusher, but I squeezed back and managed to avoid any lasting damage. I already knew he was stronger than I was.

He finally went, after giving me his cabin number "in case you want to call it off." Turned out his was directly above mine, two decks up. Which explained how he got assigned to our boat.

As we walked down to our cabins, Jan shook her head and said, "Men. Do you honestly think women are impressed by that stuff?"

I said I guessed not. I said I supposed it was pretty stupid. On the other hand, I remembered how it felt with Kenni holding on to my arm, and I knew I couldn't have turned this down for all of Schaeffer's money.

6

And then there was the briefing, and a totally different Schaeffer showed up. He was charming, he was gracious, he answered all questions, even the most stupid, with patience and humor. The fans loved him, and I couldn't say I blamed them.

I was sitting unobtrusively in the back of the room. I didn't really need to be there—I wasn't one of the celebrity suspects, and I wasn't one of the contestants, so I could have skipped it and milked my nap, or played with Spot, or eaten another banana from my fruit basket. I was here, I suppose, continuing my self-appointed Sir Galahad over Jan and Kenni. I guessed it was working. As Schaeffer was gracious for his fans, he occasionally sent searching looks toward our contest winners, especially at Jan (I supposed he had given up on Kenni), but he never came within twenty-five feet of them.

We were in a small auditorium. It had blue-green curtains and seat upholstery and was a dead ringer for Network Screening Room D. Except of course that Network Screening Room D was not susceptible to hurricanes. That wasn't a problem at the moment, though. The weather was still calm, and the deck concrete-solid beneath us.

Billy got up on the small stage, and asked all the celebrities to join him. He introduced them as the characters they were supposed to play in the week-long mystery, which was a 1930s missing-heir plot. All that was missing was Charlie Chan or Philo Vance, and the idea was for the contestants (split up into groups of ten) to cast themselves in those roles.

I looked out at the faces of the mystery cruisers. Some I knew from my visits to Bogie's; some were, and would remain, complete strangers to me. Karen had said people had come from as far as Seattle to be part of this. Every one of them was eager and excited. I thought of hounds baying to be let loose at the fox, and similar clichés. This murder was going to be such *fun*.

Real murders, I thought, aren't fun. They grow out of greed and fear and jealousy, and they leave you feeling dirty, even when you manage to catch up with whoever did it.

Maybe Schaeffer was right. I mean, I liked to say that murders kept finding me against my will, but the fact remained that four times now, I had found myself ass-deep in them. There was no law that required me to get involved, just a job I didn't especially like and—

And *what?* I asked myself Maybe a deeper, realer, more intense (and therefore less wholesome) form of the same excitement the people around me felt? Did I secretly enjoy poking my nose in piles of festering human emotions looking for the germ that had started the decay?

I had never thought about this before, and it bothered me. Then the fact that I never *had* thought of it before bothered me in and of itself. I'm not a *great* big fan of modern psychology, but it stands to reason that if you suppress something, you are probably aware of it. I was making myself depressed.

And while I was at it, I spent some time depressing myself with the thought that maybe everybody's favorite conceited old fart would wipe me out at Ping-Pong. What did I know? Maybe in between workouts, he rallied with the Red Chinese national team.

I sighed, then told myself to cut it out By the time I tuned back in, Billy's briefing was over, so I didn't, and haven't to this day formed, any clear idea of what that mystery game was supposed to be. It turned out not to matter.

Just before we adjourned, Billy announced the Great Ping-Pong match that night, and said he was sure everybody would want to attend. I was going to have to talk to that boy.

The next stop was the dining room First night was informal, which suited me fine, since there wasn't time to get into my tux

They had arranged a little ghetto for the mystery-writing types. I was in at a small table at the fringes of it, along with Jan and Kenni, Mike Ryerson and his wife Judy, and the fifth, and in a quiet way the most successful of all of the celebrities, Althea Nell Furst, who had written something like two hundred romantic suspense novels, all of which had the name of a bird in the title. She'd never hit the best-seller lists, but she had never been out of print, either, and there were legions of women out there somewhere who read the latest Althea Nell Furst, *TV Guide*, the *National Enquirer*, and that was it. Mrs. Furst (she was a widow) *did* look like a librarian, or the old-style grade school teacher. Her gray hair was done up on the top of her head in a bun, and she wore harlequin glasses with a string attached so she could hang them around her neck. The glasses didn't hide the twinkle in her blue eyes, though, and when Mike and I stood to seat her, she beamed on us, as proud as if she'd taught us to do it herself.

Mrs. Furst was traveling with her grandson, Neil. Neil, it seemed, had devoted approximately forty percent of his ten-year-old life to devouring action-adventure books. It turned out he was a devoted fan of all five of Mike Ryerson's identities. He kept telling Judy how lucky she was to be married to him. Judy, a charming and quiet woman with light brown hair and eyes, said she knew. Neil started to ask Mike in detail about all his books. "In Flagellator Number Seven, *Doom of Darkness*, where Dirk cuts out the mugger's heart with the steel-tipped whip—boy that was the greatest. How did you think of that?"

His grandmother smiled indulgently at him, and let him go on until the food arrived. Mrs. Furst and Mike, each in his own way, made sure Jan and Kenni were in on the conversation. Kenni was loving it. Jan and Mrs. Furst appeared to be hitting it off. They were making plans for the day the ship got back to New York; apparently, one of Mrs. Furst's major unfulfilled ambitions was to buy out a woolen shop in New York. Then Jan and Mike compared notes on Village bars, a subject of which they both seemed to have encyclopedic knowledge.

At one point Mrs. Furst took Jan by the wrist. "Excuse me for interrupting, dear, but that man is staring at you. Don't look at him now. Drop your napkin or something. Mr. Schaeffer must be quite taken with you."

Jan stared down at her Cornish hen. "I think it's Matt he's staring at, Mrs. Furst."

Mrs. Furst wore a look of scandalized glee. "Oh, goodness!"

"It's the Ping-Pong game," I explained wearily. "He's trying to psych me out."

"What does he expect you to do?" Neil wanted to know.

"Tremble? The sixth-graders did the same thing to us in the cafeteria before the fifth-grade/sixth-grade soccer match."

"What did you do?" Kenni asked.

"Stuck our tongues out at them."

I laughed. "Like this?" I said. I caught Shaeffer's eye and stuck my tongue out at him. The look on his face was worth the trip. Everybody at the table burst out laughing.

Jan asked Neil what happened in the game.

"Oh," he said casually, "they massacred us. But not 'cause we were psyched out. It was because they had a couple of retards who *should* be in eighth grade by now who kept running over us."

"What is his problem, anyway?" I wondered aloud.

"Jolson syndrome," Mike said.

Kenni giggled. "I'm sorry, I just couldent shake the image of him on one knee singing 'Mammy.'"

"That's not what I meant. I used to work for William Morris before I got fired for excessive tallness. Some of the old-timers there used to talk about Jolson. Jolson never hung around with anybody else in show business. He could be the sweetest guy in the world with his friends, but his friends were exclusively real-estate men and used-car salesmen and people like that. He avoided other entertainers like the plague. One of the old-timers said that Jolson went nuts at the idea that there was anyone else the public could love."

Mrs. Furst nodded. "You know, I wondered about that. I remembered a nice young man named Schaeffer who used to talk to me at Mystery Writers of America meetings. We got quite friendly. I was wondering if this was the same one, because he's barely said hello to me."

"Hell," Mike said, then shot a look at Mrs. Furst. She didn't seem to mind, so he went on. "I fixed him up with his first agent. We used to go to bars in the Village and commiserate when whatever coed was the current light of his life had snuffed him out. He's the only person I ever met who'd talk about Raymond Chandler whenever he was drunk."

Mike pursed his lips as though he'd reminded himself of something. He took a small sip from a glass containing a clear liquid and a slice of lime, and went on.

"And I used to look at his manuscripts. One day he handed me one that was a competent Chandler rip-off instead of an embarrassment, I gave him the name of a short former colleague at William Morris, and the rest is history.''

"How does that relate to Al Jolson?" Kenni wanted to know.

Mike grinned over the top of another sip. "Oh. Sorry. The point I was trying to make is, outside of mumbling hello, he doesn't talk to me anymore, either.''

Mike had Jan convinced. She was nodding unconsciously, as though she knew the type.

"See, when I was publishing and he wasn't, it was okay for us to be friends. As soon as he started doing the same thing I did, I was competition and it wasn't.''

"It's unfortunate," Mrs. Furst pronounced.

"Some crummy friend," Neil said. "You're a better writer than he is, anyway.''

Mike beamed at him. "Kid, I'm *five* better writers than he is. What the hell.''

"He used you," Kenni said.

"It wasn't like that. At least I don't think it was. It was Jolson syndrome. Anyway, who cares? He wasn't a happy man when I knew him, and six best-sellers and a million dollars later, he's still not happy. Besides, I've probably helped fifty writers get started, and forty-nine of them are still good friends. If foreign aid worked that well, America would rule the world. Now, Kenni, Judy tells me you've done some writing you're afraid to show people.''

Kenni said Judy had broken a promise not to tell, and she didn't want to be a bother. Mike said it was no bother, and not to blame Judy, because he beat her if she didn't tell him everything. Mike told her to pick out her favorite manuscript and send it to him.

Kenni was overwhelmed, and I was pretty impressed. Billy and Karen seemed to have cornered the market on helpful writers, what with Nicola Andrews and Mike offering to critique Kenni's stuff. Mrs. Furst said that if she'd written anything in the Romantic Suspense line, she (Mrs. Furst) would be delighted to see it, but after the first of the year, since she had an early December deadline on her own current book.

Everything was sweetness and light until dessert was cleared away (I didn't have any—big Ping-Pong match tonight) and Mrs. Furst took out a pack of Virginia Slims and a black Bic lighter.

A tall, slender black man in a white tuxedo with a red carnation in his lapel rushed toward the table. I thought he was going to be one of those lightning lighters, the guys in fancy restaurants who can get a flame under your nose faster than Billy the Kid could clear leather. These guys never fail to impress me. Every time I'm in a restaurant with someone who smokes, and one of these guys shoots a flame past my nose to light a cigarette for someone who has been perfectly capable of lighting twenty-six of her own so far during the course of the day, I make it a point to say, "Whoa, am I *impressed*."

He wasn't there to light Mrs. Furst up, at all.

"I am so sorry," he lied. "That is not allowed."

"I beg your pardon?" Mrs. Furst said.

"Smoking is not allowed in this section."

Mike said, "What about them?" He pointed to the people at the next table, who were happily puffing away.

"That table is in the smoking section."

"But I was supposed to *be* in the smoking section," Mrs. Furst said. "I specifically said so in my reservation."

"I'm sorry, madam, but it was not possible to seat you in the smoking section." He kept smiling. His smile was fierce, almost angry. He had a pointed face, and his medium-length Afro had retreated to a sharp widow's peak. He looked like a black Satan. And he was enjoying this.

"But she specifically requested it," I said.

"But she also requested to be with the writers, sir. She was the only one who smoked. I thought she would be cooperative." The usually musical lilt of a Davidian accent couldn't hide the scorn in his voice. This was shaping up to be a hell of a cruise. I was meeting either people I liked a lot, or people I couldn't stand.

"You fall into the latter category," I said.

"Sorry?"

"It should be a simple matter to adjust the boundary of the smoking section to include this table," I said.

"Quite impossible, sir, I'm afraid. It would be an imposition on the rest of the people in the no-smoking section. Perhaps madam would exchange seats with someone."

"Why don't we ask the other people if they mind?" Neil suggested.

The satanic smile widened. Neil shrank back. "That would put them on the spot, wouldn't it." It wasn't a question the way he said it.

"Mrs. Furst," Mike said sweetly. "May I have your permission to punch this officious jerk?"

Mrs. Furst was becoming exceedingly embarrassed. This, of course, is the weapon of the rude—the good taste of the polite. "Please," she said, "no."

"Then," Mike went on, "may I please have a cigarette?" He looked up into the grin and matched it. "Let's see you bully me into putting it out." I happened to know Mike had spent six miserable months kicking the habit two years ago, and like a reformed alcoholic, hadn't touched a butt since. Apparently, this clown got on his nerves as badly as he did mine.

It wasn't smoking. I hate smoking; I'm not crazy about being around smokers. I literally will not touch a cigarette with my fingers. But this guy was taking such delight in ruining a nice old lady's meal, was being so ecstatically uncooperative and gleefully obstructive, *I* was almost ready to choke down a lungful of Virginia pollution just so I could blow it in his face.

"Who makes the seating arrangements?" I asked.

The smile widened. "I do."

"And who the hell are you?"

"Watson Burkehart, Acting Chief Dining Room Steward."

"Acting, huh? Enjoy it. The president of the line is going to get at least one letter telling him just how you're acting."

Smile never wavered. "I have my duties, sir."

"And don't hold your breath waiting for a tip from this table." No words, just more grin.

Then I saw something from the corner of my eye. Lee H. Schaeffer was watching this as if it were an episode of the "Newlywed Game," or something equally embarrassing. And his grin was as wide as Mr. Watson Burkehart's. Maybe wider.

"Then tell me this. How much did the gentleman give you to ruin our meal?"

The grin slid from his face like an egg from a Teflon griddle. "I don't know what you're talking about," he said.

"I just bet you don't."

"Please," Mrs. Furst said. "Let it go. I really should quit smoking in any case. I only started because Eleanor Roosevelt did, and I admired her so—"

Jan didn't hear her. Or, if she did, she wasn't prepared to let the matter drop. She, too, caught a glimpse of Schaeffer's grin (and, I thought, damn if he *isn't* staring at her), set her lips, put her napkin down, and got up.

She stalked over to the other table, smiled radiantly at Billy and Karen and Phil and Nicola and the rest, just to show this wasn't a table-to-table feud, then bent over Lee H. Schaeffer and put a few low, but intense words in his ear.

I could read his lips as he responded, "There, there." He tried to take Jan's hand.

She showed him where. She smacked him across the face with her other hand. Mike and Neil cheered out loud. Mike said, "I always used to tell him—*don't touch.*" The rest of us smiled. I reflected that if my forehand was as good as Jan's, the Ping-Pong match would be a snap.

7

". . . The thrill of victory; and the agony of defeat—
The human drama of athletic competition . . ."
                    —Jim McKay
                    "ABC's Wide World of Sports" (ABC)

I walked into the gym humming "Sloop John B." I'd been doing it for hours, but I wasn't sure why.

I looked around at the gym and was impressed. It wasn't big enough to have a decent full court basketball game in, but the ceiling was high, the lights were good, and there was enough run-back room to have a decent game of Ping-Pong. There were even little bleachers along one wall for people to sit in, and sit they did. In surprising numbers. I decided these cruise lines have a racket—here these people had paid hundreds of dollars to be entertained for a week, and their idea of a good time first night out is to watch two amateurs play table tennis.

Kenni and Jan were not here yet—they were stowing Kenni's prize away in the cabin. Yes, the luscious librarian had won another contest, folks, this time in her own name.

It was actually quite a clever little mystery. The disco had been renamed the Enquiry Room for the occasion. The Bogie's customers, and anybody else who wanted to, entered, read the sign that said THIS WAY TO VIEW BODDY, then were led past a sheet-shrouded form on a table. The form was that of a young man named Bob Madison, who has been hanging around various mysterious functions since he could take the subway by himself, and probably held the record for portraying Bogie's corpses. When the sheet was lifted, a really remarkable job of effects makeup was revealed. Bob had a bullet hole between staring eyes, and a stab wound in his chest. He was tied up like a silent-movie heroine about to be placed across the railroad tracks. There was a stain at the back of his head that matched the red stain on the piece of pipe that lay beside him. The light from a single candle cast an eerie light on the whole business. I could almost believe he *was* dead—until I walked past him, and the staring eyes recognized me and he gave me a wink.

Having seen the body, everyone was now hot to question suspects, but there were no suspects to question.

"You can get all the information you need," Billy announced, "speaking to each other, being polite and introducing yourselves to the waiters who will soon be circulating among you, and thinking hard about a famous clue. The victim had a house party; each guest prepared a dish—which will now be served to you—and the killer is the odd one out. Have fun."

This sort of thing separated the sheep from the goats in a big hurry. Half the crowd said huh and scratched their heads and gave up, and half got into it and really began to think.

For those who were actually looking for a challenge, it was an added fillip that Billy and Karen had not told the mystery writers about this, so they were just as in the dark as anybody else.

I didn't play. I got a glass of orange juice from the bar, found a chair in the corner, and defended it against all comers. Table tennis puts a remarkable strain on legs and feet, and I wanted to give them every chance. I might have looked, even to myself, a little silly, compared to Lee H. Schaeffer, who was working the waiters as if his chance of heaven depended on it, but it's who looks silly after the game that counts.

Besides, it didn't make that much difference. All six of the waiters were very conscientious, bringing their wares to every corner of the room. I did play along with the game sufficiently to introduce myself to each of them, and to find out that all of them claimed the name "Parker." When I asked them about it, they replied, smiling or grave, that they were sextuplets.

The food they brought around was quite whimsical, too. Each Parker sextuplet had just one kind of food on the tray. The first one who came by had marshmallows. The second had little sandwiches, mustard and cress. The third had chicken wings. The fourth had peeled and sliced kiwifruit, which, I was given to understand, was becoming a major crop on St. David's Island. The fifth had strawberries, and the sixth had prunes.

I didn't take anything—I would eat at the midnight snack buffet after the match, if I was still showing my face in public—but it occurred to me that if you ate all that other stuff, you might need the prunes.

A couple of people from Chicago came by, and asked me what I thought of such shenanigans. I told them that with some of the shenanigans I had pulled, I had no right to judge. We discussed shenanigans.

Kenni made her way through the crowd and came up to me, very excited. "I've got it!"

I introduced her to the couple from Chicago, then asked her, "Got what?"

"It's a Clue game."

"We've got a Clue game, too," the couple from Chicago said. "The kids love it."

"This puzzle here. It's a Clue game. That's the key. Billy said to remember 'a famous clue.' The waiters are the Parker Brothers. The sign spelled 'body' wrong, but 'Mr. Boddy' is the victim in a Clue game. Also, he was killed with a *lead pipe*. And there are all these other weapons."

"Well, don't tell me, tell Karen or Billy, before somebody figures it out and claims the prize."

"Oh," she said. "Good idea. Thanks. I'll be right back," and left.

The lady from Chicago wanted to know if we were engaged.

"Lord, no," I said. "We just met today."

The husband said, "Talk about shenanigans," and his wife gave him an elbow in the ribs.

Anyway, since Kenni had figured out the hard part, it was easy to see who the killer was. Everyone prepared a dish, and the killer was the "odd one out." Okay. Miss Scarlet did the strawberries, Colonel Mustard did the mustard-and-cress sandwiches, Mr. Green did the kiwis, Mrs. White did the marshmallows, and Professor Plum brought the prunes. Mrs. Peacock brought neither peacock nor something blue. Therefore, she was the killer.

And that's the way it turned out. Billy announced the contest was over, and that there was a winner. Kenni won a huge stack of books autographed by the authors on the cruise. When he asked her how she figured it out, she just said it was easy. Billy reminded everybody that the main mystery, to be solved by one of the teams officially registered for the mystery—sorry about that folks, but there was a lot of Bogie's Murderous Mystery Tour literature available if you're interested—might begin at any time, but he would advise everyone to be sure to be at breakfast tomorrow.

Somebody who told me, in the middle of my vacation, which (I reminded myself) this was supposed to be, that I was advised to get up for breakfast, even if I didn't feel like it, was likely to get a resounding "up yours" as a reply. The revelers, however, took it with great excitement and anticipation.

I headed over to congratulate Kenni, and to help carry her books home, but Phil DeGrave intercepted me en route. "That was a rotten thing you did," he told me. His tongue bulged his left cheek.

"What was that?"

"Giving your girlfriend the answer to the mystery so she could win the books."

"What the hell—?" I ran a hand through my hair. "Phil, there are so many things wrong with that I hardly know where to begin."

"How about," he suggested, "saying you just met her today, and she's not your girlfriend."

"That's good," I said. "Or the fact that I didn't *know* the solution to the mystery. Kenni came over and told me. I've got witnesses."

"Bah," Phil said. "A put-up job. You told her long ago."

"She's a librarian, for God's sake. Why would she need to cheat to get some books? Are you playing one of your obscure intellectual games, DeGrave, or is someone actually saying this contest was a fix?"

He grinned. "Oh, someone is actually saying it. A little old lady—not part of the tour—who has been going to St. David's Island since before all these disgusting *tourists* discovered it. She had it on *good authority* that it was all staged. She would not reveal the authority. To paraphrase Rex Stout, I express no opinion as to who it might be, but boy, I sure have one."

"This stinks," I said. "This is really making me angry."

Phil nodded. "Forget what it says about you or Kenni, it makes Billy and Karen out to be liars. And that could ruin their business."

I said, "Mmm. I hadn't thought of that, but you're right. They said no one but the two of them knew the solution, but for me to have told Kenni, they would have had to tell me. What's he got against Billy and Karen, for God's sake? They love him. Billy was collecting that asshole's books before anybody. He even takes some of his stupid bread in the restaurant."

"I don't think he's thinking. Or maybe he's a psychopath, and doesn't give a shit about anybody but himself. Maybe he's trying to get you upset and put you off your game."

"Maybe," I said. If Phil was right, Schaeffer was making a big mistake. I always perform better when angry. It comes of being a young white boy haunting Harlem playgrounds because that's where the best basketball was. It wasn't until I'd taken a few elbows across the eyes that I'd gotten mad enough to forget that these kids had no special reason to love white people and a lot of resentment to work off, especially resentment against a white boy who could go back to a decent neighborhood when the sun sank. When I got angry, I could forget all that, and show them I could play the game. And through the game I got respect.

I took a deep breath. "Perhaps," I said, "a few words with him will be in order."

"I thought that myself," Phil said, "but Nicola convinced me it would be better if she did it. On account of the fact I'm about ready to slug the guy."

"You?" I demanded. "What about me?"

"You," Phil said, "are going to get the opportunity to feed him a Ping-Pong paddle. I'm counting on you."

"Good," I said. "More pressure. Just what I need."

"No pressure. Just remember that if you lose, no one will ever speak to you again."

"Thanks."

"Anyway, I just wanted you to know why people were giving you the hairy eyeball, if you run into any."

I told him I appreciated it, and went to my cabin to walk Spot and change for the match. Kim had remade the bed I'd slept in, and turned down both. Force of habit, I guessed, or he figured Spot was such an aristocratic dog he slept in a bed. There was a chocolate on each pillow. I've always wondered about that. Chocolate is fat and sugar and caffeine. Just what you need before going to sleep. I ate them both for energy.

This was about the time "Sloop John B" started running in my head. I kept coming back to the line "This is the worst trip I've ever been on."

The cruise director was a guy named Vic Ramis He was, in public, at least, bouncy, witty, patient, and absolutely impossible to get a negative word out of. The Catskills and the Poconos are full of guys like this, usually guys who didn't quite have the drive to make it as stand-up comedians. They fascinate me. Anybody who has to be nice all the time fascinates me, probably because I could never do it. What do these guys do? Go home and throw darts? Beat their kids?

Vic had agreed to referee the match. He called us over to the table, and I got my first look at Lee H. Schaeffer in shorts. He had muscles on those long knobby legs, not surprising, considering the running and skiing he did. He was wearing gray shorts and shirt, just dark enough so I couldn't say he was wearing white for me to lose the ball in, and a baseball cap that had a patch on the front reading "Rocky Mountain Ski Club."

Vic seemed a little embarrassed. He spoke sotto voce. "Uh, how legal do we want to play this thing?"

"Don't you know the rules?" Schaeffer demanded.

"Yes, Mr. Schaeffer, I know the rules, but a lot of times guests don't . . . stuff like no finger spin on serves and things like that, and they resent it if you try to tell them. So we can do this nice and easy, where I just call did it hit the net or what, or I can enforce everything."

"The rules are what make the game," I said. "Enforce them."

Schaeffer glared at me, as if angry to hear me saying something he agreed with. "That's fine with me," he said.

Now Vic was really embarrassed. "Well, in that case, Mr. Schaeffer, I don't know if that baseball cap is strictly G.I., if you know what I mean."

I suppressed laughter. No sense psyching Schaeffer up with anger this close to the match. "Let him wear it," I said. "I'll be wearing a sweatband, if I can turn one up." I had brought one, but it was white. Jan and Kenni were seeing if they had one. It occurred to me that Schaeffer needed the baseball cap for more than just keeping sweat out of his eyes. His coiffure, carefully constructed of hairs and hair spray, and blow dried into submission to cover a bald spot, would not survive the rigors of the match.

Vic asked us if we wanted to rally a little to warm up. Schaeffer said he was willing to, if I needed it, but I said no, thank you. Why show him anything before the match? Vic clasped us by the shoulders and told us to shake hands. We did, because everybody was looking. Then he spoke to the crowd, introducing us, saying it was a special challenge match, best two out of three. (I had tried to get three out of five, but had lost out in pre-match negotiations.) "And may the more proficient gladiator," Vic concluded, "emerge victorious."

Vic then flipped a Davidian fifty-cent piece. Schaeffer called heads and won. He chose first serve. I took the end of the table with the door behind me, figuring that a broken background might prove a slight distraction for him.

Vic said we'd start in two minutes. I went over to talk to Jan and Kenni, who were just taking their seats. Kenni looked distraught.

"We couldent find a sweatband. Well, only a little pink one."

"I'm confident enough in my manhood to wear a pink one," I said.

"I diddent bring it."

I was about to say there was no harm done but Jan got in first. "I've got a scarf. A cotton railroad bandana, you know. You can roll it up and tie it around your head just like a sweatband."

What the hell, I thought, if Schaeffer could wear a baseball cap, I could look like Cochise. Jan pulled a flaming red railroad bandana from her pocket (already rolled up—this was a confident woman), told me to turn around, and tied it at the back of my head.

"Time, gentlemen," Vic said.

Jan and Kenni insisted on giving me kisses for luck; just a couple of quick pecks, but I figured it might bubble Schaeffer's blood a little.

I turned to go. Jan said, "Matt?"

I turned back.

"Before you go out there, Kenni and I want you to know we think you have *great legs*." She grinned. Kenni was grinning and blushing at the same time. I was still smiling when I reached the table. Good, I thought, give Schaeffer something else to wonder about.

He took the ball and served. Nothing fancy, just sounding me out. I tapped it back to him. I could tell by his stance, by his grip, by everything about him, that Schaeffer was a smasher—someone for whom the game consisted of hitting a little white ball four hundred miles an hour and watching people try to hit it back.

I love playing against that sort of player, the kind with the Chinese penholder grip, and the tendency to run around their backhands, being careful not to slip on their drool whenever you put a high one across.

Because my game is to return everything and beat these guys with their own impatience. The longer you play, the better it works.

Schaeffer hit a forehand drive, I chopped it back. He hit a backhand drive, I chopped it back Eventually, he had me fifteen feet back from the table, chopping back his drives six inches off the floor, but he still wouldn't put a change-up on me This was a man who probably knew a macho way to put on his socks.

I have to admit, he was good He won the first game 21–16, and practically all my points came on shots he sent long, or dribblers off the net.

After the game, we switched ends, and I served first. I lost the first two points, and started to get mad at myself. Just to change my luck, I gave him a backhand serve It didn't travel as fast as a forehand, or skim the net as low, but it had a tricky bit of sidespin on it

Schaeffer hit it back over my head The crowd, which had been politely silent up till then, made a little noise. Schaeffer slammed the edge of his paddle down against the table Vic looked alarmed, but Schaeffer got hold of himself I gave him another backhand, which he whiffed on completely. This upset him so much that when I came back with a standard serve on the fifth point, he hit it straight into the net. The service changed with me up 3–2.

I was up 8–5 when I decided it was time He put down a forehand drive with just a little less topspin on it than usual, and I got my left hip and right shoulder into it, and shot it by him.

By world standards, it wasn't much of a smash. It wasn't as good as his. But we'd been playing for over a half hour now, and he hadn't seen one from me, and he had undoubtedly decided I couldn't do it at all. He looked hatred at me, a hatred that intensified when I did it again on the next point. This time, he hit the ball wild. One of the spectators got the ball and gave it to me I bounced it casually across the table to him.

"Your serve," I said mildly.

After that it was easy. Schaeffer suspected he was being made to look like a fool, and so made a bigger fool of himself than I ever could have. He sprayed balls around worse than Gerald Ford on a golf course. He kept cursing under his breath, fouler and louder as the match went on. The people watching, most of whom had started out as fans of mine, and undoubtedly knew me as the cheater of the mystery game, wound up rooting for me.

I won the second game 21–17, and the third 21–6. The last point had to be especially maddening, since it was a bad shot on my part that hit the top of the net and dribbled over.

Schaeffer smashed the paddle into the table so hard, he broke it. He didn't wait around to shake hands. He didn't even wait around for Vic to announce the final score. He was striding for the door, practically sprinting.

"Just a minute," I said. "We had a bet."

Schaeffer paused at the top of a stride. I could see the back of his neck turn brick red as he remembered what the bet was. Then he started walking again.

"That's all right," I told his back. "You don't have to say it. You're demonstrating it."

He stopped again. This time he turned around. There was anger in his face, but there was anguish, too. I had gotten Mr. Sensitive Macho where he lived. He *knew* he was an asshole, and he knew that everyone in the room knew it, too. And there was nothing in his "code" to tell him what to do about it.

He turned away and hurried from the room. I think it was to get away from everybody before the tears I saw welling in his eyes had a chance to spill.

Jan and Kenni had joined me by this time. The looks on their faces told me they'd seen the tears, too.

"God," I said. "Almost makes me feel sorry I beat him."

"But not quite," Jan said. She was smiling. In my experience, women have a much healthier attitude toward a triumph over an asshole; i.e., if he deserved compassion, he wouldn't be an asshole.

"No," I said, "not quite. Let me take a shower, and we'll hit the late-night buffet. I'm starving."

8

"This is true stuff One hundred percent true "
—Bob Saget
"The Morning Program" (CBS)

I knocked on the door Kenni asked who it was

"Just me," I said "Matt."

"Oh Just a second " The cruise line was very security minded It took a good half minute before she could undo all the locks and latches "Hi," she said. She had taken her makeup off—I could tell only because her lips and eyebrows were a little bit lighter than I was used to seeing. She still looked terrific

"Jan went to the disco," she said.

"Not you?"

"She went to meet guys. I'm not interested in the kind of guy you meet in a disco."

She had a paperback book in her hand, marking her place with a finger. I asked her what she was reading.

She showed me It was *Bloodwhip*, Number Six in Mike Ryerson's Flagellator series I asked her how she liked it.

"It's *good*. It's *funny* I never would have—I mean, even though I won it, I probably never would have looked at it if he haddent been so nice Also, I wondered why Althea Nell Furst was so calm about her grandson's reading his books."

"Satire."

"Exactly. Even when it's raw, it's not pandering."

"You should read Number Fifteen."

"I probably will, now. Why?"

"He trashes the Stephen Shears books It's funnier now that I've met Schaeffer "

"You trashed him tonight "

"I wonder, though."

"What about?"

"Is this going to make him more or less obnoxious over the days we've got left?"

"He couldent *possibly* be more obnoxious," Kenni declared. "It's silly standing in the doorway like this. Come in."

Kenni and Jan's room was a mirror image of mine. I took the chair at the desk; Kenni sat on the edge of her bed. Her back was very straight.

"I just came by," I said, "to ask you how to wash the scarf. I mean, I would have done it in the sink with a bar of soap, but I didn't want to ruin it."

"You don't have to wash it."

"I am not," I told her, "Elvis Presley, that I should give people my sweat as a gift."

She giggled. "Just throw it overboard, then. Jan's got a dozen of those things."

Then we ran out of conversation for a while. It happens when you're getting to know someone. It's always awkward. To break the silence, I said, "I'm going to take Spot around the deck. Care to come along? The book will be here when you get back. It's not like you have to bring it back to the library or anything."

She laughed and said, "Sure. Just let me get my jacket."

Since she was back in this morning's beachcomber outfit, with an impressive length of leg showing, I didn't know what good a jacket would do, but I just said, of course. Judging from what I see in New York, women train their legs to be impervious to cold.

We got Spot, who was delighted to see Kenni again, then went up to the boat deck, figuring that would be the quietest, and walked around.

There was a breeze, now, and peaks of white foam were visible as far as the lights of the ship could reach. If you thought about it, you could feel the ship rocking slightly.

"I wonder how long it's been since we've left calm waters. Schaeffer will undoubtedly claim the rocking of the waves put him off."

"Let's not talk about Schaeffer. Since I set foot on this ship, he's been making life miserable."

"Good point. Now that you mention it, I'm sick of him myself. What do you want to talk about?"

Kenni went to the rail and looked at the water. Rock and forties pop from different dance floors inside fought for possession of the Atlantic night air. "I have to confess something," she said.

I hate when people do that. "I have to confess something" or "There's something I have to tell you." While they wait for the invitation to go ahead, I'm always busy imagining all sorts of horrible possibilities. Right now I was thinking she was about to tell me she was in fact a spy from the New York Public Library, sent to collect twenty-seven thousand dollars in overdue fines for some book I had taken out as a kid and forgotten.

That's not what it was.

"I looked you up," she said.

"What do you mean, you looked me up?"

"In the *New York Times* Index. Then on the microfilms of the papers. When I found out you were going to be escorting us instead of that disk jockey."

"Joe Jenkins," I said. Maybe there was something to this cruise stuff—I hadn't thought of Joe Jenkins all day. I wondered how the search for him was going.

"Whatever. Anyway, I thought your name sounded familiar, so I looked you up. I couldent help myself. I'm an awful snoop."

"Yeah," I said. "Spot, bite her."

She stepped back. "What?"

"A joke, Kenni, relax. My stupid way of trying to tell you I am not offended by snoops. Considering what I do for a living, I wouldn't dare."

She smiled. We started walking again. Walking was now something we had to think about some; the deck was likely to be closer or farther away than you thought when you tried to step on it. I was impressed with Spot. He had twice as many feet as we did, and it didn't faze him in the slightest.

"I'm sorry I jumped. I should have known Spot wouldent bite anybody."

"Oh, he'll bite people. On the throat, even. He's been well trained. It's just that 'bite' is not the magic word."

"What *is* the magic word?"

"I can't tell you."

"Oh," she said. "I guess I understand."

"No, you don't," I assured her. "I can't tell you because Spot is here. If I say it, he'll do it, and you ·wouldn't like that."

"Great, now even your *dog* intimidates me."

"He's not exactly my dog, and what do you mean 'even'? Are you trying to say I intimidate you?"

"Of *course* you do. My God, Matt. You've caught actual murderers! I lied before when I said I diddent know that."

"That's Schaeffer's hang-up."

"You're vice president of a giant corporation!"

"Me and, at last count, a hundred and sixty-eight others."

"You were Monica Teobaldi's *boyfriend*!"

"Me," I conceded, "and, at last count, a hundred and sixty-eight others."

"Matt!"

"Another joke. Sorry. I can get bitter at Monica; she broke my heart, twice. And she wasn't even a big star, then."

"Then there was Wendy Ichimi, last year."

"When I was sixteen, I necked with Lorraine Federico in the balcony of Loews 86th Street."

"Is she famous?"

"She was in my neighborhood."

"Matt! I'm serious!"

"Okay. I'll be serious, too. I'm just a guy, okay? I happen to work in television, and I meet people who have to do with television. Why the hell should any of that intimidate you?"

"I liked you. I liked your picture, and I liked what I read about you, and when you showed up this morning, and I was so stupid over the intercom, and you were so nice about it, I liked you right away."

"So?"

"So, I'm just a *librarian*."

"Just a *librarian*? *Just* a librarian? It's only the most important job in the city. The library is the escape hatch from the neighborhood, or it's the place you go to learn how to fix the neighborhood up."

"I know that. It's just so . . . unglamorous."

"Kenni, believe me, vital is better than glamorous. And let me tell you something. Since I saw you this morning, I've wanted to, how shall I put this, check you out."

"I thought those were the signals I was getting," she said. "I just couldent believe it."

I took hold of her and kissed her. "Believe it now?"

"Starting to," she said, and went back for further evidence. It seemed she *was* an awful snoop.

Eventually, we went back to my cabin to discuss it, then after a while, we stopped talking. Later, the Atlantic rocked us to sleep.

9

"Matt," she said, nudging me. "Wake up."

I opened one eye. Kenni was looming over me, peering through a curtain of soft, thick hair. I've noticed that women almost always allude with shudders to the way they look first thing in the morning, but all the ones I have been privileged to see under those circumstances have looked just swell.

"Again?" I said. "I'm willing to try, but don't expect too much. What kind of books do you keep in that library, anyway?"

She kissed me on the nose. She was very uninhibited for a librarian. For anybody. "I don't want to do it again."

"Oh," I said.

Kenni flushed. "I mean, I do, but not now."

"Just as well. I can rest up."

She got up from the bunk we'd shared, making it less crowded, but also less interesting. She started tugging on my arm. "It's time to go to breakfast."

"So call the steward and have him bring breakfast."

"I can't."

I rubbed my eyes. I was beginning to wake up in spite of myself. "No," I said around a yawn, "I suppose that would be less than discreet, wouldn't it? Okay, *I'll* call the steward, and order a great, big breakfast, and you hide in the bathroom when he brings it. Or I'll order two of everything, and say half of it's for Spot. Although Jan undoubtedly knows you didn't get to your cabin last night, she's not going to think you suddenly got an urge to hit the casino room. I think . . ."

"Are you always like this in the morning?"

"You've got the rest of the trip to find out," I said, and she blushed.

"We've got to go to breakfast in the *dining room*. Remember what Billy Palmer said last night?"

"No," I lied.

"Something to do with the mystery is supposed to happen at breakfast this morning."

"Oh, all right," I said. "We don't have to wear a tuxedo to breakfast, do we?"

We were the last ones to arrive at the dining room. The adversity of the night before had made us comrades, and we greeted each other warmly. I scanned the room. Watson Burkehart was standing near the far wall, as far from us as it was possible to get, and if he had any brains he'd stay there.

Jan cooed her hello, and greeted Kenni and me with a knowing smile that I found kind of irritating. Kenni blushed again. I was beginning to think she probably blushed when she peeled a banana.

Mike Ryerson had an elbow on the table, holding his chin up. His eyes looked like the circle-of-red, circle-of-white, center-of-blue device the RAF paints on the wings of their airplanes. Neil Furst, who this morning was sitting at the right hand of his idol, was looking at the man with naked hero worship.

"Mr. Ryerson showed me how the casinos work," Neil explained.

Judy Ryerson grinned ruefully. "The old scoutmaster here was going to show Neil the evils of gambling."

"Now, Judy," Althea Nell Furst said. "I agreed, that since Neil seemed so fascinated, he should be shown it firsthand by someone he admired, rather than hustled on some street corner by a three-card-monte dealer. What happened was simply . . . unfortunate."

I turned to Mike. "So what happened?"

"I won six hundred bucks."

"Oh," I said. "That is unfortunate."

"I'll say. I almost feel obligated to do this every night and show him what a fluke it was."

"I just wanted to *see*," Neil protested. "I never said I wanted to gamble."

"Good for you, kid," Mike said. "If you're gonna bet, bet on sure things. Like Cobb here at Ping-Pong." He turned to me. "I would like to thank you, Matt. You added ten years of my life when you pushed in that conceited bastard's—pardon me, Mrs. Furst—stuck-up nose. Or took ten years off his, which is just as good."

Althea Nell Furst peered through her harlequin spectacles. "The conceited bastard in question—and pardon *me*, Mr. Ryerson"—she smiled—"does not seem to be here this morning."

"He's supposed to be," Jan said. "It said on the game sheet that the suspects were supposed to be here, so that they could answer questions better during the grilling sessions."

"Well," Mrs. Furst said sweetly, "he really has no one else to alienate but the Palmers, now, does he?"

It occurred to me that I never wanted to get this woman upset with me.

Food came. I'd never hit the midnight buffet last night, thanks to Kenni, and while the Food of Love is terrific, it doesn't stick to your ribs like a good corned beef sandwich. I was glad now that Kenni had insisted on coming to the dining room—I could tie into double orders of pancakes, back bacon, and home-fried potatoes without having to share. In situations like that, I am a nose-down kind of eater, and I more or less withdrew from the conversation while my tablemates discussed which of Billy and Karen's suspects was going to get it this morning, and how.

I was sitting up to arrange space for the last forkful of potatoes when the yelling came from the kitchen.

"You t'ink I don't know what you do wit dem, you crazier dan you are ugly! You sell my cookware on St. David's, you *t'ief*!" Then came the magic words. "If I still had my knives, I cut you up wit' dem."

It was as if I could see a hundred light bulbs go on over a hundred heads. *Threats*, I could almost hear them thinking. *Threats of violence. Threats of violence in a loud, theatrical voice.*

A hundred mystery buffs rose as one and went to the kitchen. I was puzzled; Billy and Karen's mysteries were famous for not depending for their solutions on someone getting an unobstructed view of some enacted event. They reasoned that everybody who paid money should have an even chance at the prize. Found bodies were much more their style than flamboyant threats.

I turned to look at the next table, realizing even as I moved my head that they wouldn't be there. Of course not. They'd be in the kitchen, making sure everything went according to plan.

But there they were, solid in their seats, looking shocked and confused.

That's when *I* went into the kitchen.

Please do not get the wrong impression. I am not the sort who rushes to the scene of trouble heedless of his own safety. If that's the kind of person I was, I would have become a fireman, the way I wanted to when I was six. I would have stayed in the army.

I went into the kitchen because Kenni Clayton, Guest of the Network and inveterate mystery fan, had been practically the first one in there, and she had dragged with her Janice Cullen, Network Contest Winner. I felt instinctively that Marv Bachman would regard either or both of them getting killed, or even hurt, as Bad Publicity. There were personal considerations, too.

I elbowed my way through the crowd, getting cursed and threatened until I said, "Let me through, I'm part of the show," in a loud stage whisper. This, I decided, was what Moses must have said to the Red Sea. I reached the scene of the action in no time.

A large fat man wearing a chef's hat and a very perturbed expression was waving a broken Worcestershire sauce bottle in the vicinity of the throat of Mr. Watson Burkehart, Acting Chief Dining Room Steward. Burkehart was leaning backward over a pile of dead, plucked ducks which seemed to be on their way toward becoming tonight's dinner. From the grimace and the drops of sweat on his dark face, it was apparent that he expected to be a dead duck himself, and soon.

"All the time you torment me, boy. Educated boy. University boy. I remember you walkin' down the street wit' a ratchet in your waist waiting for a tourist to come by, now you're a big mon in the ship, steal from Islanders, now."

He went on, saying the bloody Swedes would make him pay for the missing knives, but Watson Burkehart would pay first.

In the short time I had been exposed to the Acting Chief Dining Room Steward, I had found little to admire. He was not, however, a fool. "Clem," he said. "Clem, my old friend. I don't know what happened to your knives, but I'll help you pay for them. I'll pay for them myself."

Clem made a gesture with the broken bottle. "You say dat *now*."

"I'll—I'll pass the hat. Take up a collection."

Clem hesitated. I stepped in.

"Sure," I said. "Put me in for five bucks. Make it ten."

Clem looked at me. "Why you want to mix in? What are all dese people doin' 'ere?"

"Don't want to see you in jail," I said. "The food on this trip is too good, and I understand you're the man who cooks it."

"I can't cook wit'out my tools."

"Get new tools on the Island," I told him. "Let Burkehart go, tell the purser what you suspect. You cut him, you'll go to jail, lose your job. Is it worth it?"

"For a t'ief? No way." Without looking, Clem threw the broken bottle over his shoulder, scoring a basket in a large garbage bin against the wall. He continued to loom over Burkehart. "You get out of 'ere now, you 'ear me? You may be a big mon in the dining room, but I see you in my kitchen again, I'll run you t'rough the meat grinder."

Burkehart fled, but not before he gave me a curious look, something halfway between gratitude and suspicion. To hell with him, I thought. I got my charges out of here without bloodshed.

Clem started to laugh. It was strong laughter, strong as his anger had been.

"T'ank you, mon. I won't go to jail for the likes of him, dat t'ief. My cousin's boy; I got him his first job with the Swedes, and look how he t'anks me."

He stuck out his hand; I took it. "Why do you think he was the one who took your knives?"

"I know he did it."

"How do you know?" I wasn't trying to accomplish anything, just giving Burkehart time to make his escape.

" 'Cause besides me, he's the only one that have a key." He rubbed his chin. "You really like the food, huh? And dese people, dey like it, too?"

I turned to look. The rabid mystery fans were still there. Half of them had little notebooks.

My friends, the couple from Chicago, were nearby. I looked at the wife's notebook. She had written "Cobb likes the food," and underlined it three times.

10

"Look," I said. "I'm sorry. I was just trying to keep a real murder from happening."

"That part was a *good* idea," Karen said. We were in the Palmers' cabin up on A deck. It was midmorning, so the disco, thank God, was quiet. From the look of the two of them, they hadn't gotten a whole lot of sleep. They kept consoling themselves with the knowledge that shipboard entertainment, by law, had to cease while we were docked in Davidstown, which would give them a couple of nights to sleep, at least.

"And," I went on, "it's not my fault Clem went crazy when he did."

"Did you have to tell them you were part of the show?" Billy asked plaintively. "Every time I deny it now, I get called a liar." His tone gave the impression he didn't like it.

"I don't know if I had to. It was the first thing I could think of that worked."

"I hope this Burkehead appreciates what we've all gone through to save his worthless life," Karen said.

"Burkehart," I said.

"Are you sure?"

"I'm sure. When I dislike somebody that much, I make a note of his name. Don't you like him, either?"

Karen dropped her voice confidentially. "He gives me the creeps. I don't like people who are polite in snotty ways."

"That's interesting," I said. "To my table, he was snotty in a polite way."

61

She laughed. "Maybe you should have let him be killed."

Billy gave out with a yawn that made a nearly complete circle of his moustache, then gave out with a sigh. "The one *I* feel sorry for," he said, "is Bob Madison."

Karen started to giggle. "Poor Bob."

I asked what happened, and Billy explained. "He was our victim. Cyanide poisoning in his breakfast. Nobody noticed. There he was, blue makeup on his face, slumped over with his cheek in a plate of scrambled eggs, and nobody saw him at all."

"So what have we got here?" Karen said. "We've got a murder that's part of the game that nobody saw. They're supposed to grill suspects this afternoon, what are they going to ask them?"

"That's easy," Billy said. "They'll ask me about the totally irrelevant scene in the kitchen, which they refuse to believe is *not* part of the game. Thanks to Matt. No hard feelings."

No, I thought, just guilt.

"And if that's not enough, we've got one of our celebrity guests sulking."

"You get one guess who," Billy told me.

Time to defend myself. "Hold the phone a minute, Bill. You're the one who made the goddam Olympic Games out of a simple grudge match."

"Schaeffer told me it was supposed to be friendly! I didn't know you hated each other's guts! You'd only met five or six hours before, for God's sake."

"I was bowled over by Schaeffer's anti-charisma. What do you mean he's sulking? I didn't see him at breakfast, but what else?"

"He didn't go to Phil and Nicola's speech this morning," Karen said. "It's sort of traditional that the writers turn out to hear each other."

"The news I get is that he doesn't like other writers."

"He's done mysteries with us before—he's always gone. And he doesn't answer the door, and he doesn't answer the phone—I've even had him paged."

"Well, don't panic," I said. "I doubt he jumped overboard over a stupid Ping-Pong game."

Billy nodded, eyes wide, lips tight. "Well," he said, "if he doesn't show up in costume to be grilled as a suspect this afternoon, I'm going to drop him overboard myself. If I ever find him."

"Meanwhile," Karen said, "the whole mystery we spent a month writing is messed up. What are we going to do about *that*?"

"I have a suggestion," I said.

Billy said, "It's the least you could do," but he was smiling. That was a good sign. I've never seen him actually lose his temper, but even his *smoulder* is scary.

"Move everything back a day."

"But that would mean a grilling session while we were docked," Karen protested. "We didn't want to do that."

"It seems to me," I said, "that a bunch of people who will get up in the middle of breakfast and cram into a hot kitchen in the hope of seeing some fake bloodshed will not mind too terribly giving up an hour or two on the beach. You are dealing with fanatics here."

"Tell me about it," Billy said. Then he started to laugh.

"What's so funny?" Karen demanded.

"I was just imagining the look on Bob Madison's face when I tell him he has to nosedive the eggs again."

But not only did he dive back into the eggs the following morning, he came back from the dead to become one of the suspects in his own death, replacing the character who was to have been played by Lee H. Schaeffer, who was still making himself scarce. More than scarce. Out of a masochistic sense of curiosity I started looking around for him.

Kenni thought it was a silly idea. "If you found him, the only thing you'd accomplish is to have him back again, making everybody miserable."

I had to concede her point. "But," I said, "look at the education we're getting about the ship."

Jan would smile at this point, something that took a lot of effort on her part, because as the seas got rougher, our contest winner got sicker. "I never should have given up on airplanes," she said frequently. "Kenni doesn't want to learn about the ship, she wants to solve that stupid mystery. Whoops." Then she'd struggle to her feet and run to the bathroom, and Kenni and I would go find something else to do.

Kenni and I had already discussed that aspect of things. She'd work her way through the Palmers' mystery, but only for personal satisfaction—she wouldn't go for the prize. This time, she *did* have an unfair advantage, and I had given it to her. She knew for a fact (or, perhaps more accurately, accepted as a belief) that the disappearance of Mr. Schaeffer, like Clem's run-in with Watson Burkehart, was *not* a part of the game.

God knows nobody else believed it. Any time I tried to ask anyone if they'd seen Schaeffer, I would get answers like, "What if I have?" or "Do your own detecting." The most forthcoming response I got was from an obnoxious little twerp with acne and a pop-culture master's thesis on Food Symbolism in the Private Eye Novels of Lee H. Schaeffer in full-blown progress, who said he would sue if Schaeffer did not turn up in time to (a) give his speech, (b) sign all the first editions of Stephen Shears books the twerp had brought with him, and (c) answer about sixty-seven thousand questions about the significance to Schaeffer's character of baking muffins without tunnels or peaks. The twerp was convinced it was sexual symbolism—a subtle way of showing that when the macho man is forced into sensitivity, resentment of women must surface somewhere—but he didn't think his professor would go for it without Schaeffer's backing him up. To get the answer to this, he had spent *x* dollars for this cruise, and if he were fobbed off with writers of mere *mystery* stories, all his money would have been wasted, and he would be damned sure to get it back.

"There's probably a very good academic reason for this," I said, "so forgive my naiveté. Why didn't you just spend twenty-two cents and write him a letter?"

The twerp scratched a zit at the corner of his mouth. I was not as queasy as Jan was, but I wasn't on the greatest of terms with my alimentary canal. I wished he would stop, before I had to hit him or throw him overboard or something.

"I did," he whined. "He didn't answer. I think he must have me confused with a *fan* or something." He brought a few more fingers into play.

"That wouldn't be fair," I said conversationally. "By the way, if you pop that thing, I'm going to kill you."

Amazingly, he didn't want to talk anymore after that. He just repeated his threats and twerped off back to wherever he came from.

"You see?" Kenni said. "I *told* you I couldent understand why you want to look for that man. Even his *fans* are obnoxious."

"That's not fair, either," I told her. "Billy and Karen think he's great."

"As a writer."

"Even I thought he was okay as a writer, if you like the same old private eye story dressed up with a little eighties angst."

"Somehow, I don't think you're the angst type, Matt. You're not looking for him to ensure the world's supply of angst."

"No," I confessed. "I'm looking for him because I think he's a son of a bitch, and I think he's up to something."

A light came into Kenni's eyes. I should have told her this days ago, it would have saved me angst. Because this was different. This was a Plot, a Puzzle, and she and I were going to solve it.

"What do you think he's up to?" she asked. "Besides hiding his face in shame, I mean."

"Come on," I said. "Haven't you ever known anybody like Schaeffer before?"

"Not so bad."

"You've led a sheltered and fortunate life. Blusterers are ace rationalizers. Schaeffer made a fool of himself. He knew it, I knew it, everybody knew it. Ordinarily, that would be good for one night's embarrassment. Next morning, he'd be in sick bay, complaining of an eye infection, or he'd have a cast put on his hand. He'd put out a story of how I cheated him, and how he'd see to it that I never got the chance to hustle anybody at Ping-Pong again."

Kenni looked thoughtful. "You're right," she said. "You're right. That would be just like him. Now that you put it that way, it's weird that he hasn't done *something* like that. Something to put him back in a favorable light with his fans. I wouldent think he could live this long without his adoring fans."

"He may have some adoring fans in on this," I said. "Either that, or someone on the ship's crew he bribed, the way we think he bribed Burkehart to make our dinner miserable that first night out."

Kenni stopped walking. "Hey! Do you think Schaeffer got Burkehart to steal the knives?"

"To slaughter us all in our beds? Bunks?"

"I wouldent put it past him. Or as a cover for stolen food. Schaeffer has to eat, wherever he's hiding."

"There's no end to the things you're good at, is there? I never thought of that. I wish I could follow Burkehart around and see what that weasel gets up to, but on the ship, it's impossible.''

"But Matt, what's the *point*? He can't hide out for the whole trip.''

"He doesn't have to. Here's what I think he's up to—he hides out until we get to St. David's Island. Then he sneaks off the ship, or Burkehart or somebody smuggles him off, he makes tracks to the airport, and flies back to the States. Maybe he hangs around New York for a while, so people can see him and ask him if he isn't supposed to be in the Caribbean. He tells them he got disgusted with the food or the company, or worse, with the way Billy and Karen are running things, and he bailed out.''

"But that could hurt their business!''

I nodded. "And with a week to spread the story around unchallenged, there's no end to the damage he could do.''

"That *bastard*.'' Looking at Kenni's face, I was glad she hadn't stolen the knives.

"Relax,'' I told her. "I don't *know* that's what he's up to, I just wouldn't put it past him. But at least now you know why I want to find him before we dock.''

"So what do we do now?''

I had mixed emotions about the fact that it was now "we.'' On the one hand, it meant I had convinced her. On the other hand, it meant I was now working closely with an enthusiastic amateur whose previous investigations had all been games.

I decided to let it pass. She *was* sharp, and she might spot something. Besides,. my theory was that Schaeffer was playing a game—a stupid and nasty one, but a game nevertheless.

"What we do now,'' I said, "is to toss Schaeffer's cabin.''

"Toss? As in search? Couldent they make us walk the plank for that?''

"Nah,'' I said. "Clap us in irons is the worst they'll do.''

"Very funny. How do you plan to get in?''

"I'll get in,'' I said confidently.

"You can't break the door down. Even if you wanted to, the thing is steel. Are you going to pick the lock?''

"Not exactly.''

"You've got a master key?'' Kenni's eyes were very bright.

"I've got something better than a master key.''

"What could be better than a master key?''

"A note from the purser telling the steward on that deck to use *his* master key and let me in."

Kenni did not actually say, "Wow." Her face, however, said it for her. Now she figured I had such clout, I had convinced the purser (who is traditionally the chief investigator of crimes at sea, the captain being the judge) to deputize me to solve this mysterious disappearance.

In reality, the purser was a mild-mannered little guy, possibly the shortest adult Norwegian alive, who was tired of being bugged about mystery games. He was just as happy to humor me if I'd get out of his hair, most of which, by the way, grew in the form of a huge handlebar moustache.

As the steward let us into Schaeffer's cabin, he told me he was supposed to stay and watch us, but since Kim said I was okay, he was going to go on deck and catch a smoke. Unless we wanted him around.

I was happy to let him go. Now, in the unlikely event I found something, I wouldn't have to make a mental note of it, to be discussed with Kenni later, and I wouldn't have to worry about her blurting anything out.

I was not expecting a whole lot. As far as we could tell, Schaeffer had only been in the place one day, a short time to impose your personality on a particular set or surroundings For another thing, the steward, like a good boy, had been coming in here twice a day and cleaning up the place.

Still, it wasn't likely Kim's colleague had thrown away much. Maybe we'd find a scrap of paper tucked away in a drawer that would say, "I think I'll hide in the Engine Room, ha ha."

No such luck. Which is not to say we didn't find anything in the drawers. We found something in almost *every* drawer. Not only did Schaeffer not believe in traveling light, he was an Unpacker. My philosophy is, if I've got to stick it back in the suitcase in the foreseeable future, why take it out before I want to wear it? Schaeffer was one of those people who wanted to make every room they ever slept in into a home.

One drawer had shirts—dress shirts on the left, casual stuff on the right. Another had slacks and shorts. The third was split between socks and underwear. He traveled with an incredible number of socks. His tuxedo and two suits and more shirts were hanging in the closet, along with a pair of gray wool slacks. They all smelled of recent dry cleaning.

"You have to wonder about a guy who brings wool slacks to the tropics," I said.

"Maybe he's planning to meet someone back in New York when the boat docks. Not everybody has the panache to pull off tropical clothes in Manhattan in the autumn, you know." Kenni was smiling prettily.

"Good point," I conceded.

"Find anything?" she asked.

"Just that burn mark on the carpet," I said. "Schaeffer didn't smoke—at least, I don't think he did. I'll check with Billy and Karen."

"Doesent look like a cigarette or a cigar did that," Kenni observed. I had to agree. What it looked like more than anything was the purser's moustache, a wide parabola with the burn deepest at the peak and fading away toward the ends. It was the kind of mark you sometimes get on a garage wall when the exhaust pipe gets too close to it.

Kenni had wandered to the porthole. She looked down. "What's this?" she said.

"What's what?"

She handed me a piece of plastic, a curved triangle the same beige as the rug. It had some scratches on it—it had obviously been broken off something cylindrical. It was strong and stiff. It looked like Cycolac, the stuff football helmets are made of.

Kenni said, "That might have been there for ages. A vacuum cleaner can't get that close to the wall. It might not have anything to do with Schaeffer."

"That's it," I told her. "Cheer me down. Looks pretty fresh, though." I rubbed the burn mark and got some faint charcoal staining on my fingers. "Still gives up particles," I said. "I'll ask the steward what shape the rug was in when the ship pulled out."

"I bet Phil and Nicola and Mike and Mrs. Furst are all getting plots for novels out of this." She followed this with a sigh.

"What's so sad about that?" I said, as I dropped to the floor and attempted to look under the bunk. There *was* no under the bunk. The mattress was on a plinth that was attached permanently to the floor. I started checking under mattresses.

"What's sad about it is that *I'm* getting an idea for a plot about this, but with all those professionals in the same boat—"

"So to speak."

She smiled. "—what chance do I have?"

"They're professionals, Kenni. They're probably all in the middle of contracts. They couldn't just drop everything and write about this. If you've got a good idea and the time to do it, then *do* it."

"It might be a good idea. Could I try it out on you?"

There was nothing under the mattress of either bunk. There were no loose spots in the plinth. I put the bed back together as well as I could, but Kim's colleague would not be pleased. To Kenni, I said, "I was sort of hinting in that direction, yes."

"Well, it would have to do with Gardeno."

"Who?"

"Martin Gardeno, the Mafia guy. The one who skipped out on that indictment about seven years ago. I remember, because he was in the headlines of all the papers when I first came to New York."

"I remember, too. He was the broker behind some of the first of the show-biz cocaine scandals. But why would he be involved?"

"He lives on St. David's Island."

"Son of a gun," I said. "How did you find this out?"

She blushed. "The same way I found out about you. I always research places I'm going to go. I spend my time sitting in a library, after all. It wouldent do to let it go to waste."

"I guess not. Tell me more. You may be on to something here."

"I may?" She sounded surprised. "I've been racking my brains trying to think of a connection between Schaeffer and Gardeno. I just think the background is neat."

"Tell me the background," I said. "Maybe that will help you think of a connection." Besides, I wanted to hear the background.

"Well, apparently, Gardeno had people in the prosecutor's office . . ."

"Gardeno's type has people everywhere," I said. There was still the bathroom to look at, but it would be impolite to walk out on Kenni. I decided to toss the main cabin again while she talked.

"I suppose they do," she said. "That could be a plot element. Anyway, he knew well ahead of time that there would be a good chance he would be indicted, and he did something about it.

"Right after they got their independence, there was a lot of corruption on St. David's Island. This new group has gotten rid of it, according to our government, but about ten years or so ago, the Island was a major drug-smuggling way station. Also, they have numbered accounts in the banks here, the way they do in Switzerland and Panama. Gardeno started construction on a palatial estate on the back end of the island, paid a fortune in bribes, maybe used some threats, and got himself declared a legal resident of St. David's Island before he even came here."

"Thereby staying close to his money while he beat any extradition treaty there might have been with the United States."

Kenni smiled at me the way she might smile at a kid who had mastered the Dewey decimal system. "Exactly. Anyway, he'd make a great character, I think. Supports all the Island charities, but never leaves his estate. Maybe he's longing to get back to America, but he knows he never can. How desperate or violent will he get?"

"Sounds like the new government here could make him a major tourist attraction."

"Oh," Kenni said. "They don't like him much, but he's retired now, or at least he moves his operations through some other country. He hazzent broken any laws on the Island, so what can they do? My problem is making the leap from an exiled mafioso to the disappearance of an obnoxious mystery writer."

"Well," I said, "you are definitely destined to publish your stories."

"Thank you. But why do you say that?"

"You've got the right attitude. All week long, we've heard these people complaining to each other about plot problems. For God's sake, how difficult can a job be when you're allowed to set your own problems and make up your own answers?"

"You'd be surprised," she told me. "What do we do now?"

"Now we look in the bathroom."

Actually, I went alone to look in the bathroom—there wasn't room for both of us. The usual stuff was there—electric razor, after-shave (the one that made you "smell like a man"), toothbrush, toothpaste, dental floss, deodorant. The soap and towels and paper products were all ship-issue—nothing to be learned about Schaeffer from them.

Then there was the hair stuff. I have an uncle with high blood pressure, diabetes, gout, and seven allergies, and his medicine cabinet didn't hold as much stuff for his entire body as Schaeffer's did for his hair. There were nutrients, made of stuff like eggs and beer and placentas, things I would fight over before I let someone rub them on my head. There was a leather case containing different brushes, one square, one round, one half round. They all had ebony handles, with reddish rubber studded with porcupinelike plastic quills at the business end. Gold letters on each said "guaranteed heatproof." There was a special shampoo in a purple bottle that had more disgusting stuff in it, which apparently made it safe for "brittle, treated, dyed, and blow-dried hair." This was accompanied by a can of hair spray in a can the same color purple, bearing the same legend, adding only "nonsticky."

"Take a look at this stuff." I stepped out so she could pass.

Kenni took me up on it. She was reading how protein from placentas (I was just as glad they didn't tell us whose) was, in this particular preparation, "heat activated," when she suddenly stopped and said, "My father says hair is like money. A man never worries about it until he starts to lose it."

"Is your father bald?"

She giggled. "His head looks like an egg in a bird's nest." She thought for a second. "Come to think of it, though, I never caught him worrying about it. Of course, I *am* the youngest. I don't remember when he *wasn't* bald. Maybe he had stopped worrying by then."

I waved a hand around the bathroom. "Well, Schaeffer hasn't."

"Matt, all you have to do is look at him to know he's trying to cover a receding hairline. Why do you think he wore that stupid baseball cap at your Ping-Pong game?"

"I know, I know." I rubbed my temple, trying to stimulate a thought that wouldn't come.

"Then why are you so depressed?"

"Where the hell *is* he?"

"He's hiding out, like you said. Actually, if your theory is right, I wouldent worry. If he's going to sneak off the boat, he's got to come back here, first. He just can't abandon all this stuff. He diddent take *anything*."

"Yeah," I said. "Imagine what his hair looks like by now. But the more I think about my theory, the less I like it."

"Matt!" she said. "Don't do that!"

"Don't do what?"

"Convince me of something, then change your own mind about it."

I laughed. "You mean I always have to be right the first time?"

"I mean don't be so convincing about something before you're sure of it."

"I'm sorry," I said. "It's just that it occurred to me that he didn't have to be mysterious about everything. He could have stayed in his cabin—claimed it was seasickness or whatever the hell, walked ashore like an honest man, and flown back in a huff with no hassle whatever."

"But that way he'd have to face Billy and Karen, at least figuratively. This way, he's mysterious, he's important. Instead of asking how he could be such a jerk, they're asking where he is. Even you. Diddent he strike you as a man who had to be the center of attention, no matter what?"

"Of course he did, but he also struck me as a man who would never make himself uncomfortable unless it was something hip, like running marathons, or rubbing placentas into his head. I mean, unless the captain is hiding him out for some reason beyond my imagination, Schaeffer's got to be pretty uncomfortable out there. He can't have brought many clothes with him; and he can't be in the passenger areas of the ship, or else Bogie's Bloodhounds would have found him. It just doesn't add up."

Kenni said, very quietly, "Maybe he did go over the side."

"Get serious, will you?"

"Well, I heard how he just lost a girlfriend. And you did make him look pretty darned bad . . ."

"Just cut it out, okay?" I said.

"All right, Matt, I was just considering the possibility. I thought that's what we were supposed to do."

"You will excuse me if I resist considering the possibility that I drove a man to suicide with a Ping-Pong paddle."

"Oh, Matt," she said. "Even if it's true, you shouldent hold yourself responsible. I mean, just *that* couldent do it. In one day, you saw how sick a person Schaeffer was. *Is*, is, I mean is. It's like he's going to come back and haunt you, for crying out—"

Just then, the ship lurched, and the door to the cabin flew open with a bang. Kenni screamed.

11

"Can we talk?"
—Joan Rivers
"The Tonight Show Starring Johnny Carson" (NBC)

The steward could not have looked at Kenni more quizzically if she had just laid an egg in his hand. He looked at her, blinked twice, and said, "Sorry. Door slipped."

"It's okay," I said. "We were just telling ghost stories."

He shrugged. His face said he'd had crazier passengers than this. "A lady wanted to come to this room. Says she knows you. I told her I check first."

Jan's voice came from behind him. "It's me. The Dramamine they gave me finally worked, and I was going stir crazy in the cabin."

"She's okay," I told the steward. Graciously, he bowed her into the room. "By the way," I said, "what's your name?"

"Chiun," he said.

"It is not!" I said.

He grinned at me. "You're right. I read that name in a book. Some big, important Korean have that name. My name is Kim. One-third all the cabin stewards on the boat named Kim. One-third all Koreans named Kim. In Korea, it works fine, not so good on the ship. Passengers get confused. Tips go astray."

I handed him twenty bucks. "This won't go astray." While he was smiling I asked him about the burn mark on the floor.

The smile went away. "I bust my ass, sorry ladies, to keep cabin clean, but passengers are careless. I'm not responsible for that burn."

"Nobody says you are."

"Ha! You don't work for cruise line."

"I just want to know if it was that way from the last trip, or if it's new since we left New York."

"It happened Saturday night. Saturday evening, I come in to turn down beds, no burn. Sunday morning, I come to clean cabin, big mess. Worse than now. I ran the vacuum over it couple times, get up a lot of loose stuff."

"Okay, thanks. We'll be out of here in a minute."

He put the twenty in his pocket and smiled again. "Take your time. Remember to close door tight when you leave, so it locks."

"Well," Jan said brightly as I closed the door behind "Chiun," "have you found him, yet?"

"No," Kenni said gloomily. "We've just lost him worse."

"Kenni," I said, "it was just a *theory*. Theories are like tissues—you use them up and throw them away until you don't need any more."

"What do we do now, then?" She was asking that a lot today.

"Well, you two are supposed to grill suspects in the Bogie's mystery." The ship gave another lurch. "I am going to go ask for some Dramamine for myself."

Jan laughed at me. "It takes a little while to work, but it's worth it. You may want to sleep it out."

I did in fact sleep for a little while, right after I took the seasickness pills. Lying down, I think, helped as much as the medicine did. It was a strange thing, but the same motions that were so nauseating when I was trying to stand up were actually pleasant when I lay on my back. The secret was to inhale as the ship went up, and exhale as the ship went down. It made a nice rhythm. When I began to miss Kenni, I knew I was getting better.

I have this strange time sense—I always know within ten minutes or so what time it is, even if you wake me up in pitch blackness in the middle of the night. However on this trip, something had happened to me that had never happened before. We slipped over from the Eastern Time Zone to the Atlantic Time Zone, which is one hour *ahead* of New York. Since no part of the United States, but only parts of rural maritime Canada, Caribbean islands, and the east coast of Brazil are on Atlantic time, I had no practice adjusting for it, and was therefore an hour behind myself.

Right now, for instance. Spot (who doesn't give a damn what the clock says) decided it was time for me to fill his bowl again, and woke me up. I figured it was about a quarter after two, which suited me fine. Lunch (which I was in no shape to grab) would be about over, and I could ambush Watson Burkehart by the door of the dining room, where he would be standing, smiling at those passengers he had not yet offended.

I checked my watch, though, and saw three-sixteen, and now I didn't know where to find him. I sighed. The only thing to do was go looking. I arranged a meal for Spot, who tucked into it as if eating with the floor jumping under you like a teeter-totter was a gourmet experience, and got to it.

It wasn't hard to find him. The cleanup crew in the dining room told me he'd be in his cabin in the crew quarters. I wasn't supposed to go into the crew quarters—sailors having somewhat unfortunate reputations, this particular cruise line had draconian nonfraternization rules concerning passengers of either sex. However, I waved the letter with the purser's signature on it giving me the run of the ship to look for Schaeffer, and the doors were opened.

All except the door to Burkehart's cabin. The crew did not travel in the luxury the passengers did. I would not go so far as to say the hallway I was standing in was grubby, but it certainly wasn't homey. It reminded me of the heating and air-conditioning plants in the basement of the Network.

I knocked again on Burkehart's door. Hatch. With the frills gone, I could understand now why they were called hatches. "I know you're in there, Burkehart."

"Go away," he said. "I don't have to talk to you. You aren't even supposed to be here."

I decided it was impractical to try to get him to read the purser's note through the iron of the hatch. Instead, I said, "I wasn't supposed to be in the kitchen, either." A Norwegian in blue work clothes carrying a wrench the size of my right arm walked by and grinned as I said it.

"The *galley*, I mean. I wasn't supposed to be there, either. I just showed up and stopped Clem from cutting you up into tubesteaks."

"Clem was drunk. Clem is always drunk."

"Drunk goes away. Scars are forever. Look. I've got something to say to you. I'm going to say it, standing out here yelling where everybody can hear it, or in your cabin like civilized human beings, if you can manage it. It's up to you. You will notice that no one has tried to make me go away."

I think it was the insult that got the hatch opened as much as anything. Whatever it was, Burkehart opened up, scowled at me, and made me scuttle sideways past him into a room about one-quarter the size of my cabin, decorated in Early Pipe and pinups. I sat on a wooden chair. Burkehart took the edge of the bed.

He was a different man out of a tuxedo. Dressed as he was now, in slacks and a sleeveless undershirt, he looked skinny and furtive and scared. He looked exactly like the kind of guy you'd expect to steal kitchen utensils from his employer.

"So," I said conversationally. "Where's Schaeffer?"

He showed me his beautiful teeth in what was supposed to be a defiant grin. I didn't buy it. The truly defiant do not play nervously with their chest hairs while they try to put the message across. As it was, he wasn't even good at making it clear what the message was. Was he trying to make me believe he knew but wasn't going to tell me, or was it simply that he was pretending to take pleasure in the idea that I didn't know?

I put the question to Burkehart. "Which is it?"

He had about seventeen chest hairs, all coiled tightly against him like springs from the inside of ballpoint pens. Without looking, he would stretch them out, then release them, and let them coil up again. It was fascinating to watch.

So was his face. He was putting so much effort into the grin the corners of his mouth were trembling with muscle strain. He finally spoke to me, more, I think, to give his mouth something to do than to convey information. In any case, he certainly avoided conveying any information.

"It will take a better man than you to find him," he said.

"Why?" I said. "Did you kill him and dump him over the side or something?"

That killed what was left of his smile. "Get out," he said.

"To go back to yelling through the door? Just when things are getting interesting?"

"You are persecuting me," he said. "Just because I wouldn't let the old lady smoke."

"For not letting the old lady smoke you get no tip. I'm collecting the debt you owe me."

"What do I owe you?"

"You owe me for keeping Clem from scooping off your chest with a broken bottle. I think I mentioned that already. What would you do with your hands without your chest hairs to play with?"

Burkehart pulled his hand away from his chest, looked at it like it was something he'd dug up at the beach, then tucked it under his thigh to keep it out of mischief.

"Clem is a drunk. He makes threats."

"You looked like you believed him. Or do you always wet your pants at nine-thirty in the morning?"

"I did not wet my pants!"

"You were close. What did you do with the knives?" I don't know why I asked that. Instinct, I guess. When people start getting indignant at accusations that are patently untrue (I *knew* he hadn't wet his pants. They were white pants.), it's frequently a good idea to follow up with one that you think *is* true.

"I didn't take the knives. Stop plaguing me about the knives!"

"Don't get so excited, my dear Watson."

"You are going to make me lose my job." He was morose now. Everybody always picked on poor Watson.

"You're not too good at it, anyway," I told him. "You lack warmth. Where's Schaeffer?"

"I have an old grandmother to support. And children. They'll starve if I lose my job."

"Stop, you're breaking my heart. You'll need money, right? To tide you over while you look for another job. To open a little cutlery shop, maybe."

I knew from Burkehart's eyes that if he had stolen the knives, he sure didn't have them now. If he had, he would have cut my heart out with one of them, or maybe several.

"How much?" I asked.

"Five thousand dollars American."

Now I grinned. "Dream on," I told him. "I couldn't give you that if you took travelers' checks."

"You can get it. You work for a rich American company. You can get the money."

"Maybe," I conceded. "We get to the Island tomorrow."

"We will get there soon after sundown. They wait till daylight to enter the harbor to make a show for the tourists. We'll be close to shore. You could swim it."

"Well, guess what? I'm not going to swim past Customs,

Immigration, and the Coast Guard in the dark to get you money. I haven't even said I'm giving you money at all. What am I supposed to get for it?"

"You'll get your money's worth," he promised. "I'll tell you everything."

And that was as far as he'd go. He wouldn't even give me any idea of what "everything" entailed. Ordinarily under those circumstances, I'd tell him to get stuffed. Instead, I told him I'd think about it.

It was a mistake, as I found out very soon, but it wasn't a *stupid* mistake. I had reasons. Burkehart was scared, and I wanted him scared. He undoubtedly suspected that if he told me what he knew, I could use the information to neutralize whoever or whatever he was afraid of, but he was such a thoroughgoing sleazeball he wouldn't pass up the opportunity to squeeze a few bucks out of somebody even for the sake of his own peace of mind. If he'd grown up in Manhattan instead of St. David's Island, he could have gone into the New York Real Estate Market and named buildings after himself.

I wanted Burkehart scared, but I wanted him to have hope. I didn't think Schaeffer was going to swim ashore, either. We wouldn't be in the dock until eleven o'clock tomorrow morning. I'd get to Burkehart before then and see how tender stewing in his own juice had made him. One thing he didn't know was that I wasn't going to hand out any five Gs of the Network's money to him or anybody like him. If the information was good, I might come across with a tenth of that.

If I had read him right, he would have taken that and been glad to get it. I never did find out.

I reported developments to Kenni and Jan, then didn't catch up with them again until dinner. Having had my seasickness relieved, I was incredibly hungry. I took the lamb in ginger sauce with new potatoes and green beans.

The conversation was about the mystery game. I asked Mrs. Furst how she enjoyed being grilled.

"It was quite interesting. I'm supposed to be an heiress, you know, and I have the most wonderful motive—I'm tempted to ask Billy and Karen if I can use it for one of my own books—but no one asked me about it."

"What did they ask you about?"

"About you, and how you liked the food."

"And how he gets along with the chef," Judy Ryerson added. "I didn't know whether to come out of character to explain that wasn't part of the mystery, or just claim ignorance. My character doesn't know anything about it."

"I was sitting next to Bob Madison," Mike Ryerson said. "A lot of people asked him if he'd had plastic surgery." He grinned ruefully and went back to his duck.

Nobody rose to the bait. Lee H. Schaeffer had disappeared from our ken, and it was tacitly agreed that for tonight at least, he'd disappear from our conversation.

We talked about the Island, instead. I contributed the Network's interest in all this, but Jan and Kenni carried the ball. Kenni, because in addition to looking up the histories of exiled Mafia figures, she had also turned up all the stats on the Island. And Jan, because as a stewardess, she'd been there before.

We found out from Kenni that St. David's Island was about the same area as Manhattan, but had less coastline because it was round. Like Bermuda, it had originally been colonized by the survivors of a slave-ship wreck, and the races were so thoroughly mixed for so many generations, nobody gave a damn about it anymore.

"She's right," Jan said. "Of course, it may change if the tourism really takes off, but when I was there before, everyone was natural and friendly. Also, something to look for, you've never seen so many black people with bright blue eyes in your life."

"I've never seen *any*," Neil Furst said. "Until Grandma brought me to New York, I don't think I ever saw any black people at all."

Jan didn't know what to do with that; she was rescued by the arrival of dessert and coffee. Kenni went on. "There's fresh water on the island, but it has a lot of sulphur in it, so they use ground water for industry—"

Mike wanted to know what industry.

"There are significant guano deposits on the eastern end of the island. Tourists tend to stay away from there."

"You'd think so," Mike said.

Kenni drank some coffee, looked at it, made a face, drank more. I already knew she was a coffee addict, having seen her at breakfast.

"The population is about thirty-five thousand, so there's plenty of room for everybody. They trap rainwater for drinking—something else they have in common with Bermuda."

"There's practically no crime on the island," Jan said.

"Oh?" I said. "I'd heard it was a major dope-smuggling center at one time. I heard there's a lot of Mafia money in numbered bank accounts."

Jan gave me a blank look. "Oh," she said at last. "Of course. I meant, you know, *crime*. The kind a tourist has to worry about. Mugging. Purse snatching. Things like that. The Islanders don't even rob each other."

"The leading cause of death—" Kenni said. She put down her empty cup. "The leading cause of death is motorbike accidents."

"That's true," Jan said. "They drive those things like maniacs, so be careful crossing streets. Kenni, honey, are you all right?"

I had been about to ask the same question. Because she definitely didn't look all right. She was wobbly and bilious, but I didn't think she was seasick. Seasickness creeps up on you, a little at a time; it doesn't hit in the middle of a sentence.

Kenni wobbled a bit, and opened her mouth, but not to answer the question. Instead, the coffee made a return appearance, followed by dinner, and she slumped to the floor, splashing her hands in the mess as she went by.

"Sick bay," I said. "Where is it?"

"It's on this deck, just the other side of the slot machines."

I scooped Kenni up and ran. As I went by, I heard murmurs and the sound of notebooks flipping open. I heard one voice say, "Don't tell *me* he's got nothing to do with the solution."

I wanted to stop and kick him a few times, but I was in a hurry.

12

"And you slump into the Valley of Fatigue . . ."
—Welch's Grape Juice commercial

"She'll be all right," Dr. Sato assured me. He was undoubtedly the handsomest man on the ship. Apparently, he was the best dresser, too, since I had bounced in on him in the middle of a private meal in his quarters off the sick bay, and found him sitting there in his dress whites, just daring ginger sauce to mess him up. He saw me, left the meal in midbite, told me to put Kenni (who was woozy, but not unconscious) on the examining table, and threw me out.

Fair enough, I thought. He's the expert. I turned to go.

"Oh, Mr. Cobb," he said. I wasn't surprised he knew who I was. He probably had a notebook with my food preferences in it, too.

"Yes?"

He pointed to a white knob on the wall. "Turn that halfway to the right on your way out, will you?"

I walked to it, wondering what medical marvel I would be assisting in. Then I turned the knob and heard Frank Sinatra music.

He smiled a beautiful smile at me. "Patients find it very soothing, and I am a great, great fan of his."

"Oh," I said. "Good."

"She'll be all right, Mr. Cobb," he said. "This happens frequently." With his trace of Japanese accent, he sounded even more competent than he would have otherwise. A few cars, a few transistors, and those people have brainwashed an entire nation into thinking they can do anything. In this case, I hoped it was true.

"Okay," I said, "it happens frequently. What is it that has happened?"

"With the patient's permission, I will tell you when I have treated her." He smiled, bowed, and retreated. In the process, he somehow managed to get the door to the waiting room closed with me on the other side.

I sat down and looked at a week's worth of the ship's newspaper. I dwelled especially on Tuesday's. "Giants 35, Eagles 3." That was all it said. Not a single detail. I had had to wait two days for it, and I *still* didn't know anything. The next time I have anything to do with a Network contest, the prize will be a satellite dish.

I was thinking all this foolish stuff because my brain kept leading me around to a conclusion I didn't like: *someone had poisoned Kenni.*

And it could have been anyone. With all the comings and goings and table-hopping those mystery mavens went through, any one of a dozen people, not counting waiters and kitchen help, could have slipped her something.

The coffee narrowed it down a little, but not much. I had fallen in, as I frequently do, with a table full of those people who like to sit on an uncomfortable chair in a restaurant with high heels or ties on, shmoozing about things and nursing coffee or (in the case of Althea Nell Furst) cigarettes until I want to apply for a grant from the Hemorrhoid Foundation.

It didn't matter, then, that Kenni's coffee had tasted funny, since the coffee had been there as long as the whole meal before it had.

And as long, I was beginning to think, as this examination was going to take. Despite my semifamous time sense, I was astonished when I looked at my watch and saw that only a little over twenty minutes had gone by. I waited another half hour, looked at my watch, and saw that a total of twenty-five minutes had now gone by. It was a Japanese watch, so there couldn't be anything wrong with it.

I laughed at that, then sat there calling myself an asshole, laughing while a woman I was, if not in love, at least in *fond* with, was being examined by an Oriental Sinatra freak after having been poisoned.

I was expanding on the theme of my assholiness (*how did I let myself get into this in the first place, why did I ever get into macho games with Schaeffer, where the hell was Schaeffer,* etc.) when the door opened and the doctor emerged, wafted in by a few bars of "The Summer Wind."

He didn't wait for me to say "Well," for which I blessed him. I hate people who make you beg for it.

"She'll be all right," he said.

"You keep saying that," I said. My nails were making dents in the palms of my hands, but I was not shouting. "She'll be all right from what?"

"Shipboard chemical cocktail. People on the mainland take all kinds of pills—tranquilizers, antidepressants, diet pills, sleeping pills. They come on the ship. There's lots of good food so they take more diet pills. Or there's so much going on, they take sleeping pills to knock themselves out immediately when they get back at last to their cabins, instead of unwinding naturally. The body chemistry is confused from the new schedule and the time changes, and the chemicals don't help. Top it off with some seasickness, or a seasickness remedy, and the body rebels. That's all."

"Kenni hasn't taken any pills," I said.

"She told me she has taken Dramamine this afternoon," the doctor said. He frowned. "Though why she should deny taking anything else is beyond me. She must have had barbiturate at least."

"Maybe somebody slipped it to her."

Sinatra started on "Strangers in the Night." Dr. Sato hummed along for a few bars, then smiled gently at me.

"Mr. Cobb," he said. "I know you have been . . . *close* to the young lady for several days, but can you really say she hasn't been out of your sight long enough to be able to take a few sleeping pills?"

He had a point. I hadn't even known she'd taken anything for seasickness. I was too upset, though, to concede it. "Why would she deny it?"

"Perhaps she is embarrassed. Perhaps she obtains them without a prescription. I am not accusing—I am simply suggesting possible reasons a person might deny having taken such medication. It happens frequently."

"Have you handed out any barbiturates on this trip?"

"As it happens, no—though I don't think your question is quite proper, Mr. Cobb."

"Excuse it, please. I was just thinking that if Miss Clayton *has* been poisoned—"

"By whom?" the doctor demanded. "Why?"

I ignored him. "If she *has* been poisoned, whoever did it had to get the stuff somewhere."

Dr. Sato laughed in time with the opening notes of "That's Life." "Mr. Cobb, sleeping pills are among the most commonly prescribed drugs in the world, certainly in America, next only to tranquilizers and diuretics. 'Whoever' might have gotten them anywhere. Not, however, on the *Caribbean Comet*."

"Okay, fine. What happens to Miss Clayton now?"

"She is very weak; she will sleep now. Upon awakening, she will perhaps have a headache. I have told her to come see me if that is the case."

"Come see you? Aren't you going to keep her here?"

Dr. Sato bowed. "I made such a suggestion. She greeted it with scorn. When I said she should be kept under observation, she said you and someone named Jan could observe her as well as anyone. With that, I must concur. It is merely a precaution, and this Jan person, I was given to understand, was once an airline stewardess, so her training should be adequate to what's needed. We have a wheelchair available to see her back to her cabin. Or wherever."

"Fine. You just keep observing her for a while. There's something I have to check out first."

He looked concerned. "I trust you will return before eleven o'clock, if at all possible."

"What happens at eleven o'clock?"

"I join the ship's orchestra in the main lounge. I sing Frank Sinatra songs." He gave me a few bars of "The Summer Wind." He sounded pretty good, except for a little trouble with the words "blowing" and "across." I told him I hoped to be back in plenty of time. He let me in to see Kenni. She started trying to get up, but I pushed her back and told her to rest for a couple of minutes. She didn't like it. Either she resented Dr. Sato's implication that she was lying about what medicine she had taken, or she just couldn't stand Sinatra. I'd ask her later. I'd ask her a whole lot of stuff later; right now, my overpowering urge was to have another chat with Watson Burkehart, on the off chance that he had arranged this as a subtle way to add urgency to my quest for five Gs to give him.

On analysis, it didn't make a whole lot of sense, but I was pissed off, and I wanted a piece of somebody, so I avoided analysis. I used the purser's letter to get me into crew quarters, and went straight to Burkehart's door, figuring since he had copped out on tonight's meal by saying he was sick, he was bound to be stuck in his cabin.

No answer. I tried a few other doors, met a few members of the crew. I learned two things. Nobody knew where Burkehart was, and nobody much gave a damn.

I tried one more door and ran into my friend Clem, the cook. He did not seem a lot more sober than he had the last time I saw him, but he still thought I was great. I had hardly finished telling him I was looking for Burkehart, who was supposed to be in his cabin but didn't answer the door, when Clem got to his feet, roared down the hall, and with a meaty shoulder, popped the hatch open.

Well, I thought, that's one way to make sure. I ambled along behind.

"The bloody bugger," Clem said alliteratively. "He's done a bunk."

I gestured for Clem to move some of his bulk so I could take a look. Clem, still on his *b* kick, said "The bastard," then moved aside.

The cabin was empty, and the porthole was standing open, wasting the ship's air-conditioning money on the muggy Caribbean night. Moonlight on wave crests made a path right to a silver beach that was my first look at St. David's Island.

I remembered Burkehart telling me how easy it was to swim from the ship's current position to the island. It had to be that much easier, now.

I took a look around while Clem, with obvious glee, went to tell the purser the Acting Chief Dining Room Steward had jumped ship. Unlike Schaeffer, Burkehart had taken stuff with him; clothes, wallet, things like that.

Then I reminded myself that Schaeffer had disappeared in the middle of the ocean, hundreds of miles from anything to swim to, and that he was too broad in the shoulders to even *dream* of slipping through a porthole, and stopped worrying about finding subtle differences.

When Clem got back, I headed back to sick bay to get Kenni. I was confused and frustrated. Before Dr. Sato went back in and closed the door, I could hear him singing "That's Life."

13 _____

". . . Fun and adventure wait for you on this
mysterious isle . . ."
——Theme song, "Treasure Isle" (ABC)

So the ship docked in the morning. Passengers, who had apparently
been dying to wave to *somebody* since the ship pulled out of New
York, gathered on deck to wave to the brightly clothed Davidians,
smiling all the while. The brightly clothed Davidians (presumably the
ones who weren't on the back side of the island, working in the guano
plant) smiled and waved back. I couldn't blame them. When
someone has spent something over a thousand bucks just to get to you
to buy souvenirs, it's bound to bring a smile to your face.

I saw the welcoming throng through the porthole of my cabin. I
was still looking after Kenni, who insisted that she was now fine, and
wanted to get in on the fun.

"Isn't it fun to pet a pedigreed Samoyed?" I demanded. "He's
certainly enjoying it. Have a little consideration for your fellow
creatures. I don't even know if I'm allowed to bring him on shore."

Kenni wanted to know why not.

"Rabies and distemper quarantine. In England, you have to keep
the dog locked up for six months to make sure he's okay."

Kenni was petulant. "Well, I'm okay *now*."

"Sure," I said. "Lying down in an air-conditioned cabin. But it's
eighty-eight degrees and humid out there. You just relax. You can
have fun this evening."

"I don't know why I let you boss me around. I'm not even the
person who won your damned contest."

I grinned. "You're beautiful when you pout. Childish, but beautiful."

"I am not childish." She folded her arms across her chest and looked at the wall. Then she got a flash of how she must have looked, and started to laugh.

"That's better," I said.

"But Matt, I'll probably never get a chance like this again. I don't want to miss the whole trip because I got an upset stomach."

"Remember what the doctor said?"

She rolled her eyes. "*Him.* He thinks I OD'd on a drug cocktail, for God's sake. I never took a sleeping pill in my life."

"You took the seasickness pill?"

"I told you that. Everybody else was feeling it, so when I got a little twinge, I took some. It's not a big deal."

"No," I said. "The big deal is that there *was* barbiturate in you. Not a fatal dose or anything, just enough to make you sick."

"How do you know that?"

"Because between us, we pissed off Dr. Sato with our skepticism. He scraped some vomit off your skirt and ran a test on it. He sent me the results. No doubt about it."

"But I diddent *take* any!"

"I believe you," I told her. "Which means someone had to slip them to you."

"You mean someone tried to *poison* me?" Her voiced squeaked a little when she said "poison."

"Well," I said, "yeah. Whoever it was didn't try too hard, considering the dosage Dr. Sato figures you got, but I would have to say a person slipping another person goofballs unbeknownst probably doesn't have the recipient's best interests at heart."

"But that's *ridiculous.*"

"I agree."

"Huh?"

"It's ridiculous. Just like it's ridiculous for a well-known man, a celebrity surrounded by adoring fans, to vanish on a ship in the middle of the ocean. It's ridiculous for Watson Burkehart to have greased his hips and slithered out through a porthole when he thought I was going to pay him five thousand dollars to tell me where Schaeffer is. And it's ridiculous that every time I drop my fork in the dining room, a hundred maniacs whip out their notebooks and write 'Cobb drops fork; picks it up with left hand.'" I rubbed my head. "At least that part's innocent. The rest is pretty damned sinister. Especially the part about slipping drugs to you."

The tip of Kenni's tongue peeped out of the corner of her mouth, and she nodded in concentration. "I'll tell you something else that's ridiculous. And sinister."

"What's that?"

"The knives."

"What about them?"

"They were stolen."

"I know they were stolen. Burkehart practically admitted he'd done it."

"That's not the point. If this were a mystery story, or the scenario for one of the Palmers' mysteries, and somebody stole a whole set of razor-sharp knives and butcher's tools, wouldent you feel gypped if nobody turned up stabbed? It's just, I don't know, unsatisfying."

I sighed. "Yes, my dear," I said. "In a mystery story it would be most unsatisfying. In real life, though, you have to take things where you can find them."

"I see what you mean," she said sadly. "For instance, if I'm going to have any fun today at all, I'm going to have to find it right in this room."

"They've got crossword puzzle books in one of the stores," I offered. I was feeling a little like a jailer, keeping Kenni locked up because I couldn't catch up to anyone who'd actually *done* anything.

"I don't want to do crossword puzzles."

"Oh," I said. "Well, anything I can do, let me know."

"All right, then," she said. "Lock the door. The hatch."

I shrugged, and complied.

"Now put Spot in the bathroom and come over here." She spread her arms and grinned.

I couldn't help but grin back, but I said, "After what you went through last night, I don't know if it's a good idea to have me bouncing around on your stomach."

"I guess you're right," she said glumly.

"Yeah," I said.

"So," she said, "I'll just have to bounce around on yours. Now get the hell over here."

Sometime later, Kenni had convinced me of her recovery. Now she was telling me she was hungry.

"Of course you're hungry," I said. "You haven't eaten anything since last night, and that didn't hang around too long."

"Don't remind me," she said. "What are we waiting for?"

"Huh? Oh, nothing. Let's go eat on shore."

"*No*," Kenni said sarcastically. "You mean I *don't* have to wait until tomorrow to see this island after all?"

"Sometimes the patient knows best, after all."

"This is more like it. Give me ten minutes back in my cabin to put on something nice."

"Be careful," I said.

She gave me a kiss on the cheek as she walked by. "You're sweet," she said.

I watched her walk down the hall, just making sure she made the twenty feet or so of hallway safely. I was sweet, but I was also nervous. We were going out because of something else I wasn't reminding her about. Someone with access to the ship's dining room had shown something less than concern for Kenni's welfare. Until I knew what the hell was going on, I wasn't keen on letting her back in there. Of course, she might get a bit hungry on the trip back to New York, but there were a couple of days before I had to worry about that.

Tonight, we would get dressed, leave the ship, take a stroll through Davidstown, make sure we weren't being followed (Kenni didn't have to know about that part of it), pick a restaurant at random, and go in and eat. I was getting a little peckish, myself.

I gave Spot a dose of affection, then filled his bowl for him. It would be another evening alone for the pooch, and I felt guilty about it. I also felt weak and kind of stupid for not having resisted Kenni's lewd advances long enough to do what I had planned to do and find out if I could bring Spot ashore. It would have been nice to have him, in case somebody decided to try something less subtle than poisoning.

I had no reason to think anyone *would*, mind you. I had no reason to think *anything*. The real case sometimes seemed just as much a fantasy as whatever the Palmers' guests were up to. More. They at least had Bob Madison's body to look at for clues.

What did I have? One burn mark. One piece of Cycolac. One set of missing knives, which, as far as anyone could tell, had not been used for anything. One missing jerk of a mystery writer. One missing sleazeball of a dining room steward.

And one nasty, but not especially deadly act of poisoning. And maybe possibly perhaps one missing disk jockey.

Oh, Matthew, I told myself, come now. What could *he* possibly have to do with it?

Well, how the hell should I know? What did *anything* have to do with anything?

I was going nuts. I had in the past, as Lee H. Schaeffer had been inordinately impressed to find out, been involved in a few messes that I had been able to name the person responsible for. But in those cases, I always knew I *could identify the mess*.

My time sense told me Kenni had been gone twenty minutes; my watch said twenty-one. She'd said she'd be gone ten. Under ordinary circumstances, I should wait another fifteen minutes at least before I started to worry. These, however, as I'd just finished explaining to myself, were far from ordinary circumstances. I gave Spot one last hasty pat on the head and hustled down the hall to Kenni's cabin.

It was Jan who answered the door. "I just got back from the beach," she said. I had already deduced that from the short, white terry robe she had on, and from the pinkish sand still clinging to her sandaled feet.

Before I could say anything, she called back over her shoulder, "It's him, Kenni." She turned to me and told me to come on in and have a seat.

"She decided to take a shower," Jan explained. I could hear the water running. "I was just about to come down the hall and tell you."

"No problem. Did you have a good time?"

"Fan*tas*tic. I never realized before how great the beaches here were. I rented a motor scooter—"

"With all those maniacs on the road?"

She grinned. She was more animated and happy today than I'd seen her yet. "I stuck to the back roads. Anyway, I found this beautiful beach on the north side of the island and had it completely to myself. I hope your friends forgive me when I say I like beaches a lot better than mysteries."

"They won't mind."

"I feel like such a fraud, being the winner of the contest."

I told her not to worry about it. Jan obliged by changing the subject. "Kenni looks great. I was so afraid for her last night."

"You're not the only one."

"Kenni says you think someone tried to poison her."

"Someone did poison her. He just didn't kill her."

"He?"

"Or she. I was being grammatical."

Jan shuddered. "There's a crazy person on this ship."

I smiled. "There are probably a hundred crazy people on this ship."

She didn't find it funny. "I mean for all this weird stuff to be happening. Some maniac or something."

"Could be," I said, though I didn't entirely agree. Homicidal maniacs, for all their faults, usually have the virtue of consistency. They decide if they want to be shooters or stabbers or stranglers or poisoners or bombers and stick with the decision until they get caught or find a new hobby. What had been happening on the *Caribbean Comet* was crazy enough, but there was a purpose to it; I could feel it. The person behind all this was working toward some goal, at which point he (or she) would stop.

"It's a shame," Jan said.

I thought so, too, and almost said so. Then I realized that since I hadn't been speaking aloud, and Jan had shown no evidence of ESP, she had to be talking about something else.

"What's a shame?" I asked.

"Kenni's been so happy up to now." She lowered her voice. "You've been really good for her, Matt. Really."

"I like her." I said it a little warily.

"Even if this is just a shipboard romance you've been good for her."

"Thanks. To answer the question you didn't ask, I don't know exactly what it is. For a minute I thought you were volunteering to be maid of honor."

"But she's got four sisters!" Jan laughed. "Besides, we don't really know each other all that well. We just live in the same building and have the occasional cup of coffee together, you know how it is in New York."

"I know how it is. Of my two closest friends in the world, one lives way upstate, and the other lives in Nebraska. In New York, I have acquaintances."

"Exactly. Not that I mind, really."

"Still," I said, "you know her well enough to think I'm good for her. Whatever that means."

"Oh, well," Jan said. "You don't have to be best friends to talk about *men*. And I've seen some of the guys she goes out with." She shook her head.

"What's wrong with them?"

"They're exactly the kind of guys you'd expect to ask a librarian out."

"Accountants," I suggested. "Clerks. Computer programmers."

"Nerds," Jan summed up. "It's not just the jobs they do, it's *them*. I mean, they're stereotypes, but Kenni isn't. She's bright and funny and I think she's always longing for adventure."

"I think she got more adventure than she needed last night."

"I'm not talking about that. I'm talking about you. You work in a glamour industry, and you've been in the newspapers. You're— you're dashing."

I cracked up. "Me and Errol Flynn."

"Well, you are. And it's done wonders for Kenni's ego to think that you've known Monica Teobaldi and Wendy Ichimi and now, for a week at least, you're paying all your attention to her."

Gee, I thought, in different ways, I've bowled over Lee H. Schaeffer and Kenni Clayton in the same week. Wonderfulness can be a curse.

I was going to expand on the topic, but the shower stopped, and I didn't want Kenni to hear how good I was for her. Jan called out and told her I was here. Kenni sang back that she was sorry for the delay, but that she'd be just a few minutes, and would Jan hand her in her stuff. Jan complied, the bathroom door closed again, and we could hear a buzzing noise. I started, puzzled, but all it was was a hair dryer.

"Would you like to join us for dinner?" I asked Jan. "We're just going to walk around and find a place."

"No, thanks," she said. "I'm just going to take it easy. Got a little too much sun today, I think."

"Will you do me a favor and check in on Spot from time to time, maybe play with him?"

"Why don't you bring him with you?"

"I never got around to finding out if it was allowed."

"It must be. I saw a lot of passengers coming and going with their dogs. There's just a guy in the customs building who checks their shot tags."

"Thanks. That's an even better favor."

I went to get Spot, figuring this would give Kenni a chance to finish getting dressed outside the steam of the bathroom. It's a funny thing. Kenni had probably dressed and undressed an equal number of times in front of Jan and in front of me during the course of the week, but all of us instantly knew that it would be weird if she did either in front of both of us at once. There are different kinds of intimacy, and they don't mix.

Spot looked at me hopefully as I came into the room. He seemed to suspect that this wasn't just another jaunt around the deck for sanitary purposes when I snapped the lead on his collar. When we left the cabin without my having taken some paper to blot him up with, he was sure of it. By the time I met Kenni at her door he was ecstatic, wagging not only his tail, but the whole rear third of his body.

The load of the ship and the level of Davidstown Harbor were such that the gangplank was placed on our own deck, about a hundred feet from Jan and Kenni's cabin. We gave our names to the ship's officer at the port, he checked us off a list, and down the plank we went.

The farther south you get, the less twilight there is. What there was of it in Davidstown, though, was beautiful. It made the pastels of the bustling town even softer, and lights twinkled a welcome. There was a fresh, gentle breeze off the Atlantic, and it made the palms and myrtles dance as it carried the fragrance of unfamiliar flowers to us. Even the cannon in the harbor park, which, according to a plaque on a marble pedestal in front of it, had seen real action against real pirates in the seventeenth and eighteenth centuries, seemed friendly somehow—as if it knew that the visitors to the island these days were here not to take loot, but to leave it behind them.

"It's beautiful," Kenni breathed. She didn't look so bad herself, in a low-backed white dress and a string of pearls.

"Glad you like it," I said, as though I had personally arranged for the harbor here to be lovely instead of the greasy slums most waterfronts were.

Spot was too well behaved to try to break loose and frolic in the grass, but by God, he wanted to. I made him a promise to find some place for him to run free while he was here.

Tonight, however, was not going to be the night. Tonight he would walk with us to a restaurant, wait patiently outside while we ate, accompany us if we decided to take a stroll under the subtropical moon, and see us safely back to the ship, keeping his lithe body and sharp teeth ready at all times.

That was the plan. I am not good at plans. Or rather, I'm fine at plans, they just never seem to work out.

We crossed the small park and went into a small but ornate structure of brick, with concrete pillars and pediments that turned out to be what is usually called the customs shed.

The customs people were prepared to deal with a whole lot more people than they needed to process this evening. Kenni, Spot, and I had to wind our way through a maze of chains on our way to the customs desk. It almost got to be fun. En route, we passed a couple of men in uniform, khaki shirts and shorts with white pith helmets, who were making their way to the ship as we were making ours away from it. Customs men, I figured, some formality on the ship they had to take care of. We smiled isn't-this-ridiculous smiles and let each other pass. One of the men stopped to pet Spot, but still smiling, his companion hurried him along. I noticed that one of them, the one in charge, did indeed have eyes of electric blue. The contrast with his coffee-black skin was striking.

A few seconds later, we made it to the desk itself, where a milk chocolate–colored man with hazel eyes, who was wearing a uniform in three shades of green, smiled what I was already beginning to think of as the Islanders' Smile, and asked us for our passports.

"Mr. Cobb?" he said as he looked at mine.

"That's me," I said.

"Mr. Matthew Cobb of New York City, U.S. of A.?"

"Uh-huh," I said. I nodded to make it more emphatic. "Is something wrong?"

"That, I am happy to say, is not for me to determine." His hand disappeared for a second under his desk and came back filled with a small, but very effective-looking .32 revolver.

Kenni screamed. Spot growled. I told him to stop.

The customs man was still smiling. I told him this had to be some sort of mix-up.

"I sincerely hope so." He drew his head back a little so he could see who he wanted to speak to without turning his head.

"Sergeant!" he called. The man in khaki with the blue eyes turned around, saw the man holding the gun on us, and began hopping over chains to make it back to the desk. His associate followed.

Kenni kept trying to say something, but mercifully, she was too upset to get more than a series of *k* sounds past her lips.

The blue-eyed man said he was Sergeant Milton Bolt of the Royal St. David's Island Constabulary, and I would come with him.

I said sure. He had a gun, too. His smile brightened. These guys would smile if their own appendix burst.

"Take care of Spot," I told Kenni. "Go stay with Jan and take care of Spot."

She was still standing there speechless as I left her.

14

"I'm one tough gazookis what hates all palookas what
ain't on the ups and squares."
—Jack Mercer, "Popeye" (syndicated)

I wasn't as cool as I was trying to let on. It's just that it's always a good idea to behave reasonably, and, until you can't help it, to let the guy with the gun decide what reasonable is. Also, getting yourself shot is one thing, but I had a woman and a dog to worry about, too.

Sergeant Bolt led me to a late-model Plymouth with an impressive crest on the door. He graciously held the back door for me (he'd put the gun away by now), and assisted me into the caged-in portion of the car. Then he got in front and told his driver to take us to headquarters.

"You forgot the handcuffs," I said.

"You are not under arrest, Mr. Cobb. Merely assisting the police with their inquiries."

"Then why all the guns?"

"The customs man is a fool. When the new administration came in, they cleaned up the customs department of the men who had winked at the drug traffic. So now we have honest men, but fools. Once he drew his weapon, the main objective was to get him to put his away, and with a scared man, the only way to do that is to convince him to leave the shooting to a more competent man. I will apologize to your lovely companion."

"I'll pass it along. It might be a good idea for you to stay clear of her for a while."

Sergeant Bolt laughed, and turned to give me a blue-eyed grin through the grillwork. Now that we were such friends, I could ask him some more pointed questions.

"You know, I would have assisted you just as enthusiastically with your inquiries if you'd just left a note with the steward telling me to drop by your headquarters.''

"Ah, the constable and I were on our way on board to proffer just such an invitation when the customs man was indiscreet.''

"What inquiries am I supposed to be assisting you with?''

Bolt was apologetic. "It is not part of my duty to tell you that. I am merely to bring you.''

The driver spoke for the first time. "Al will tell you.''

Before I could ask who Al was, Bolt had snapped the guy's head off. Discipline was strict in the Royal St. David's Constabulary.

"There is a Detective Inspector on the case. He will tell you what he deems prudent to tell you.''

"It's about Burkehart, isn't it? What did he try to do, fence the knives?''

I could see the back of Bolt's neck tighten; he'd blown one, and he knew it. "We will have no further conversation, if you please, Mr. Cobb, and we will forget your last remark. Please remember that from here on, anything you say may be taken down and used in evidence. Do you understand?''

So it was Burkehart. Now what was that shmuck up to?

"I asked you, Mr. Cobb, have you understood?''

"What? Oh, yes. Perfectly clear. Thank you.''

Constabulary headquarters was in a small, cozy-looking building that could have doubled for a beachfront saloon in any movie or TV show set in the tropics. That was on the outside. On the inside, aside from the fact that all the uniformed men were wearing shorts, it could have been one of the smaller precincts on Staten Island. The place was even painted in New York City decor—sour-apple green.

Bolt led me to an office where one of the sexiest-looking women I ever saw was sitting at a small schoolroom desk off in a corner. I was polite and said hello. Nothing fresh. She arranged her beautiful dark face into a passable imitation of a frozen trout.

"Be seated. D.I. Buxton will be with you shortly.''

I took a seat, facing a desk. It was a comfortable seat, in a pleasant room. I'm sure word had gotten around that I was not only an American, but an American who could conceivably have a lot to say about what messages about St. David's Island got across to the potential American tourist. I had no such power, of course, but they didn't know that.

What *I* knew was that if I had been Joe Schmoe off the boat, or worse, an Islander, I would be sitting in a stinky little interrogation room with no windows, literally sweating out what they were going to do with me. I also knew that there is not a cop in the world who likes being leaned on by upstairs.

Now was the time to be reasonable at all costs.

D.I. Buxton didn't make it easy. He walked in like an actor crossing a stage. He stopped at his desk, told me he was Detective Inspector Paul Buxton, and that I was who I was. He ignored the fact that I had stood and extended a hand. Instead he sat, nodded to me to resume my seat, and repeated the British-formula warning about things being used in evidence.

I said it was fine with me. I kept looking at Buxton, hoping I wasn't staring. I hadn't necessarily been expecting him to look or be like anything in particular, but I definitely wasn't expecting him to be a blond, with a straight, narrow nose and skin pinker than Kenni's. His lips were full, and his hair was a platinum Afro that stopped just short of being wild.

He stared at *me*. This was undoubtedly interrogation technique, designed to make me uncomfortable. Either that, or the Powers That Be had ridden him really hard, and he'd decided to take it out on me personally.

I crossed my legs and smiled blandly, the picture of patience.

Finally, he asked me a question.

"Are you enjoying St. David's Island, Mr. Cobb?"

"I've liked everything I could see from the window of a police car."

"I meant when you came ashore earlier this afternoon."

"I didn't come ashore until about a minute and a half before Sergeant Bolt and the other man approached me."

"I suppose now you wish to complain about the brandishing of guns."

"Not at all. Sergeant Bolt explained most satisfactorily." There was something about talking to the Islanders that made me want to sound as British as they did. Probably a mistake. I'd have to watch myself.

Buxton cleared his throat and shuffled his papers. He was young for a Detective Inspector, about my age. I think he'd been expecting this big-shot American to be somebody loud and bombastic, somebody to whom it would be a pleasure to deliver a Declaration of No Special Favors in *This* Jurisdiction, No Matter Who You Are. Now he had the speech all prepared, and I wasn't giving him the chance to deliver it.

He shuffled some more papers. At last he said, "Why not?"

"Why not what, Inspector?"

"Why didn't you come ashore this afternoon? If you truly didn't— we'll be checking that, you know."

"I'm counting on it." I smiled at him again, just a friendly smile, nothing sarcastic about it. "I stayed aboard because I was looking after a sick friend."

"I take it, then, that your friend is feeling better."

"Very much so."

"May I have the name of this friend?"

"Of course. Her name is Mary Kenneth Clayton. People call her Kenni. *She* might have a complaint about guns being drawn. The customs man frightened her half to death."

"She was the woman with you at the dock?"

"That's right."

"She had been ill. Seasickness?"

"Poison."

Buxton's pink face reddened. "I am in charge of this investigation, Mr. Cobb, and until such time as my superiors see fit to replace me, I shall run it my way. I don't care what interests you represent, or who in the government cares to appease them, I will brook no frivolity from you. Is that clear?"

"Very clear. Feel better now that you got it out?"

"What are you talking about?"

"It's not important. Look, we can save a lot of time and trouble here."

"Murder investigations frequently take a lot of time and trouble, Mr. Cobb. *I* will be the judge of what time needs to be expended here."

I made my eyes round and said, "Of *course* you will," but inside, I was going, murder investigations? *Murder* investigations?

"Look," I said, "I plan to cooperate in every way, I swear. I *want* to. I'd just like to know what's going on."

"That is the purpose of an investigation, Mr. Cobb. It is for *me* to find out what is going on, and for you to assist me to the best of your ability. You say you plan to cooperate. Fine. I would like to see some cooperation.''

This guy wasn't going to be any help. "May I please speak to Al?" I said. "Whoever he is."

Buxton looked murder at me. The shorthand-taker stopped trying to imitate a piece of furniture long enough to look at me with horror.

"What did you say?" The strain in Buxton's voice was evident.

"I—er—I just said I wanted to talk to Al. The constable said Al would explain why I was being brought in."

"Oh," he said. "Did he now?"

"That's what he said. If he made a mistake, I'm sorry."

"Oh, he made a mistake, all right, but it's nothing *you* have to apologize for, Mr. Cobb. *I* am Al. It is a name I am not supposed to know. The lower ranks like to refer to me that way. It is short for Albino."

"You're not an albi—"

"I know I'm not a bloody albino, thank you!"

I decided to play it sheepish. "Sorry," I said.

Buxton grabbed the edges of his desk, took a deep breath, and showed me a rueful smile. "Thank you, Mr. Cobb. It's not really your apology to make, but the man who owes it to me never will make it, so yours is welcome."

I saw what he meant. Bolt's driver had set me up to insult his boss for him, but if Buxton called him to account for it, it would look as if the Detective Inspector's skin was thin as well as pale.

Now Buxton stood up, came around the desk, and offered his hand to me. I rose and took it. We returned to our seats.

"This island," Buxton said, "has a long history as a society and a short one as a nation. It is our boast that our people are so thorough a mixture of black people and white that no racism is possible. That boast, Mr. Cobb, is not true. The capacity of human beings for racism is apparently limitless. I am no colonist here; there are as many Africans in my ancestry as in any man's on this island. It is my misfortune that in my family, the European genes happen to predominate. I am, as the phrase goes, 'white looking,' and no one will ever let me forget it."

"It happens in the States, too. I heard some clown at an affiliates meeting say he turned a black applicant down for being too light. He said, 'If I've got to hire niggers, dammit, I want everyone to *know* they're niggers.'" That remark got back to top Network brass (I made sure it did), and Tom Falzet, the President of the Network, replaced the guy within a week with one of the black people he'd turned down. It's nice, every once in a while, to see justice done.

"It just proves my point; white people in control or black, the actual manner of the racism remains the same. But we're getting off the subject, aren't we?"

I supposed we were. I said, "Okay, I said I'll cooperate, and I will. I guess you'll eventually tell me who's been killed."

His eyes narrowed. "Why do you think someone's been killed?"

"You *said* this was a murder investigation. They don't usually start one of those unless someone's been killed."

"I did not say it was a murder investigation."

I nodded toward the stenographer. "She's been taking down what I say, how about what you say?"

Buxton made it official with a nod. The stenographer looked back through her notes. She gave Buxton a look as sympathetic and warm as the one she'd given me had been cold. "I'm afraid so, Inspector. 'Murder investigations frequently take a lot of time and trouble, Mr. Cobb.'" Then she gave me a face of scorn for making her boss look bad. I suspected that skin-color politics might have been standing in the way of an otherwise inevitable office romance, and I felt a little more comfortable about her animosity.

Buxton showed no animosity at all. He threw his blond Afro back and laughed. "I try to be so *clever* sometimes." He laughed some more, then said, "Very well, Mr. Cobb, I will tell you who's been killed. A native of this island named Watson Burkehart."

"Ah. I suspected as much."

"Why?"

"He didn't seem like a man with a lot of friends. Also, he split the ship while we were lying offshore. He wouldn't leave a good job unless he'd been paid off or was afraid of something." I leaned forward in the chair. "I suppose you want me to tell you everything I know about Watson Burkehart."

"Yes, Mr. Cobb, I do. And I particularly want you to tell me about *this*." He pushed a clear plastic folder across the desk to me. There was a bedraggled piece of S.S. *Caribbean Comet* stationery sealed inside. There was writing on it, block printing in the smeary blue-gray ink the pens on the ship held.

It read:

I HEREBY ACKNOWLEDGE THAT I HAVE PAID $5000 AMERICAN DOLLARS TO WATSON CLARENCE BURKEHART IN EXCHANGE FOR INFORMATION CONCERNING THE DISAPPEARANCE OF LEE H. SCHAEFFER. I GUARANTEE THAT WATSON CLARENCE BURKEHART SHALL BE HELD BLAMELESS IN ANY FURTHER INVESTIGATION OF THIS MATTER, AND I SHALL MAKE NO FURTHER DEMANDS OF ANY KIND ON WATSON CLARENCE BURKEHART.

(SIGNED)
MATTHEW COBB

"That was found on his body," Buxton said. "He was killed very meticulously. He was found on a little-used beach near the fertilizer factory—"

Probably why it was little-used, I thought.

"—with his skull very thoroughly crushed, apparently with a smooth stone. Blow after blow, but judiciously applied, so as not to break the skin. Really quite amazing. I had just come from looking at him in the coroner's office before I came here. It's really something to see."

"I'd like to," I said. Buxton and the stenographer paused to give me identical dirty looks. I didn't care. From the sound of what had been done, this corpse's face was messed up. I wanted to look at it to make sure it was the Watson Clarence Burkehart I remembered. There were probably people on this island who'd known him all his life who had already identified him, including the poor, starving grandmother he'd told me about, but I didn't care about that, either. When somebody goes to a lot of trouble to mess up a dead man's head, you *have* to suspect a switcheroo. The more people who knew him well who swear it's him, the more suspicious you have to get. I didn't want to mention this. I had (unintentionally) shown Buxton up twice, and I was damned if I was going to do it again if I didn't have to.

At that, Buxton may have gotten a whiff of what I had in mind. He raised his brows and intimated it might be arranged, after he was done with me.

I tapped the plastic-covered note with my finger. "Well," I said, "now I know why you had me hauled in."

"It was indicated. I wanted to hear your explanation. I still do."

"You will notice," I said, "the note's not signed."

"I've noticed quite a bit, Mr. Cobb. Now, if you will please simply tell me what this is all about."

"Oh, God," I said. "Where do I *start*?"

Buxton looked irritated. "You might start," he suggested, "by telling me who Lee H. Schaeffer is."

Now it was my turn to laugh. "I'm only sorry he's not here to hear you say that."

But I didn't start with Lee H. Schaeffer. I went back to the beginning, to Bogie's, and Joe Jenkins, and the radio contest.

15

"And he would tell him stories of how it all began."
—Theme song, "Pow Wow the Indian Boy," "Captain Kangaroo"(CBS)

It took *hours*. Every once in a while, I'd pause for breath, or as the night wore on, for a yawn, and the stenographer would massage her hand to ward off writer's cramp.

And, strung out in a line like that, it sounded even stupider than it had seemed when I was living through it. I had more or less emptied the bag for him. I did euphemize my way around my relationship with Kenni. I mean, the whole ship knew we were sleeping together, and half of them would tell him, but I was raised always to be as much of a gentleman as I could. Buxton got the message. He didn't make an issue out of it.

". . . So we decided to go out for a safe meal, which I still haven't had, by the way—got any all-night diners on this Island?— and Bolt and friend picked me up, and here I am."

Buxton sat back in his chair, looking stunned.

"A fabulous story, Mr. Cobb. Simply amazing."

"The really amazing part is that it's all true, and I've got witnesses for practically all of it."

"Except your negotiations with Burkehart."

"Except that, yes. And they weren't even negotiations. I was just stringing him along."

"Hmm, so you said. Pity you never got a chance to reel in the string."

"I'll say. Now I'll probably never know if he was killed over something to do with Schaeffer, or some other peccadillo right here on the Island."

Buxton tightened his lips and looked at a closed venetian blind as

he debated something with himself. "That's the main reason—
Evelyn, you may go home now. Thank you for staying so late. Type
your notes up in the morning."

Evelyn gathered her things up, said good night, and left. I didn't
watch her go. It was more politic to let Buxton appreciate her by
himself. When the door closed behind her, Buxton said, "That's the
main reason I tend to believe your story, ridiculous as it sounds."

"What is?"

"The fact that Islanders do not murder each other. They just
don't."

"Clem, the chef, is an Islander. He had a broken bottle to
Burkehart's throat."

"He would not have used it. If you hadn't persuaded him not to,
someone else would have."

"He looked serious to me."

"We are a theatrical people, Mr. Cobb, not a violent one. To be a
policeman on this Island is to investigate petty burglaries and
motorbike accidents. When the word about Burkehart arrived, I
consulted the records to see when the last murder on St. David's
Island took place."

It was obvious he wanted me to ask. "When?" I said.

"Nineteen fifty-eight. A German tourist stabbed a Danish tourist
for flirting with his boyfriend." He made a face. "Before the new
hotel complex the bulk of our tourists were that sort of person."

Buxton seemed vaguely ashamed, which was ridiculous. I would
have to be absolutely mortified about living on the Upper West Side if
the very presence in your midst of "that sort of person" was
something to be ashamed of.

"I cannot find," Buxton went on, "a case of an Islander killing an
Islander with malice aforethought since 1926, when man strangled
his wife for consorting with the Devil. Even then, he was judged
insane and detained at His Majesty's pleasure."

"You've made your point. Chances are overwhelming it wasn't an
Islander who did Burkehart in. Therefore it was someone *not* from
the island."

"A tourist."

"Probably someone from the ship. We had the best chance to know
and hate him. And on the ship, we already had mysterious events."

"To say the least. And you have found nothing of Mr. Schaeffer?"

"A charred curve on the rug and a little chip of plastic. If they mean anything."

Buxton looked at his blind again. He stared at that thing as though he could see through it to some beautiful vista. Maybe he was remembering Evelyn's exit.

"You know, Cobb," he said at last, "Burkehart may have been easy to hate. Everyone who knew him was glad when he got the job with the cruise line because it would mean he would spend less time on the island. Strings were pulled, I am told, to help arrange it.

"But he was still one of our own, still an Islander. I have sent cables to New York, inquiring about you. I have received glowing replies. I know that in your eyes I am a small-town policeman with little experience and subordinates who do not respect him. Please; we will take your reassurance as spoken."

I closed my mouth.

"I intend to find the killer of Watson Burkehart. If that means I must put any number of people under bond to stay here until I do, or return here when I need them, I shall do it."

I smiled in spite of myself. I could see the hundred people with the notebooks watching Clem threaten Burkehart over the knives. I could see them told they'd have to come up with ten thousand dollars each, or they wouldn't be allowed to go home.

I could see Billy and Karen in bankruptcy. I could see Billy unleashing jujitsu. I could see a wave of murders the like of which this island had never dreamed of.

I kept my mouth shut. For all I knew, Buxton was one of the type who get stubborn when you point out flaws in their plans. And since my brain kept seeing only more and more horrible ramifications of the flaws in his plan, there was nothing to say. Buxton was showing the window how tough and dedicated he could be.

The phone on the desk rang. We both jumped.

Buxton picked up the phone, said yes a few times, then, "Shortly, Mr. Maxwell," then yes again, and finally, "I'll tell him. Goodbye."

"That was Mr. Maxwell at the American Embassy," he explained. "Some sort of attaché. He's really a DEA man, but I'm not supposed to know that. He'd like to speak to you, after you're done here. Simply phone the Embassy, and they'll send a car around."

"That's interesting," I said. "I wonder what for."

"Our unsavory past, Mr. Cobb. Your government thinks that any crime on this island must be drug-related, despite the best efforts of our new government. Since I am questioning you, Mr. Maxwell suspects you might know something about drugs."

"He's going to be disappointed."

"Hmm. Your story sounds like it was *caused* by drugs, but it has nothing to do with them per se. Still, I suggest you see the man. He can be very persistent, and if you avoid him, he'll just get more suspicious. Every time I talk to him, he mentions our numbered bank accounts. No matter what the conversation started out to be."

I sighed. "Sure," I said. "What the hell. They've got a kitchen at the Embassy, no doubt. Maybe Maxwell will whip me up a hamburger. As soon as you're done with me, I'll call him."

"That should be a matter of minutes, Mr. Cobb." He used the phone again. This time, he just said, "Results?" then grunted a few times before hanging up.

He turned to me. "Either everyone on that ship is a liar, Mr. Cobb, or you are one of the better-alibied men in the world. Dozens and dozens of people, it seems, have been taking care to study your movements."

I took a silent moment to thank God for fanatical mystery fans. I stood up; Buxton did the same. We shook hands again.

"You can use this phone," he said. "I know that number. Or did you mean it about wanting to see Burkehart's body?"

"I meant it."

"Having learned of your reputation in New York, I will admit I will be happy to have the benefit of your thinking."

I should have taken this cruise sooner, I thought. I was rapidly becoming a legend.

The morgue was in the basement of Davidstown Hospital. It was, to my somewhat jingoistic surprise, quite large, modern, and well-equipped. Especially the emergency room and the morgue. Probably because of all the motorbike accidents.

It was a short walk from Constabulary headquarters. On the way, Buxton asked me why I wanted to see the body. This time, I told him.

"Ah," he said. "But I knew the man well. I arrested him at least six times. For your theory to be tenable, *I* would also have to—"

He gave me a dirty look.

"Hey," I said. "No hard feelings. You checked *me* out."

He chuckled at that, and I liked him better than ever.

One look solved the problem, anyway. They pulled out the slab, and there was Watson Burkehart. I mean, I recognized him, but not without having to make certain mental adjustments, allowing for the new shape(lessness) of his skull. It was as if someone had painted a detailed and faithful portrait of the man on a bag of grapes.

"Nasty," I said.

"Very," Buxton said. "You can see why I want the devil caught."

"I could see why you'd want the devil caught even if Burkehart'd been hit only once."

"The coroner believes it possible that once would have done it. A smash upward to the occipital bone, you see." He pointed to a particularly deep dent in the back of Burkehart's head. "Or, if that one alone wasn't enough, that one and any one of the others."

"Right-handed or left-handed?"

"Too many blows to tell. They obliterate each other."

"Well," I said. "I've seen enough."

Buxton seemed relieved as he nodded to the attendant to cover up the body. I have this strange thing about looking at dead bodies. At the time, I'm fine. My macho glands kick in, and they overcome the urge to retch, faint, run away, etc. But they come back later and haunt me; they establish permanent residence in my memory. It was getting, I reflected, too crowded in there.

I sighed. "Next stop, the Embassy."

Buxton smiled. His next stop was home to bed, and with or without Evelyn, it seemed an attractive prospect.

"I'll ring them for you," he said.

They came for me in a big black Cadillac. It made me proud to be an American. It had little flags on the fenders and everything. Never mind that the car itself was wider than, at a conservative estimate, thirty-five percent of the streets in Davidstown. And never mind that there was a statute on the books since colonial days (so Buxton had told me) that no vehicle on St. David's Island, including bicycles, roller skates, or horses, was allowed to travel at a speed greater than twenty miles an hour. So here's a million horsepower, loaded on a boat, brought to an island that's only about fifteen times the length of the car, and condemned to drive at twenty miles an hour, scraping its sides against the buildings as it did so.

I must admit the driver did not actually scrape anything on the way to the Embassy, but there were several close calls. I know damned well he never topped twenty. Never even put it in danger. I was beginning to suspect an overzealous Constable could have arrested Buxton and me on our way to the morgue for walking too fast.

We got there eventually. I could have walked it in less time, because I could have gone down the narrow streets the Cadillac had to stay away from. The Embassy itself was a lovely old Victorian building that looked like a hotel. The driver informed me it used to *be* a hotel. Now, however, that there was the big, modern Davidstown Plaza on the bay, the hotel company had sold their stately old building to the United States for practically nothing, saying the space would be needed to serve the needs of the large influx of American tourists who would soon be arriving. They were, the driver told me, still moving in.

That was an understatement. The place was chaos, wallpaper half up (or down, it was hard to tell), cardboard cartons everywhere, scaffolding up, the smell of paint thinner scenting the night air. The Marine in the booth looked a little woozy from it. I told him I was to see Mr. Maxwell; I told him my name, he checked it on a list, and buzzed me in.

I had to duck under a scaffold to get into Maxwell's office, but other than that, he seemed to be in fairly good shape. He had his desk in place, and there were only six or seven cartons in a big room. He even had a chair for guests. Sitting in it was Kenni Clayton. Lying alongside it was Spot.

Spot usually gets browned off at me when I leave him alone too long, but this time, he seemed to understand the special circumstances. At any rate, he took a sniff in his sleep, sprang to his feet, and ran to me, giving me a few of his patented Flying Face Licks before calming down enough for me to scratch behind his ears and under his throat and generally assure him I still loved him.

Then it was Kenni's turn. I don't mean I scratched her anywhere, but I did hug back. I didn't want to make her feel like her hugs weren't welcome, even in the august confines of the Embassy.

"Matt," she said in her best thriller-heroine tone, "you're all right."

"Of course I'm all right. I was assisting the police with their inquiries, not duking it out with them."

"I read mystery stories. I know what that 'assisting the police' stuff means. It means you're about to be arrested."

"Nope," I said. "Free as a bird." Unless, I didn't say, you or I or practically anyone wants to leave the island. I'd save that for later.

Maxwell cleared his throat. Kenni blushed prettily and went back to her chair. Maxwell got me another chair from behind the cartons. We all sat down.

"Have you got anything to *eat*?" I said. "We were on our way to dinner when this came up, and it will be too late to get anything on the ship when we get back."

Maxwell may have been a DEA man, but he had enough of the diplomat in him to smile indulgently at my incredibly bad manners. "Heh-heh. Miss Clayton showed up here several hours ago, insisting I help you in any way I could. I have to admit this wasn't on my list of ways. But I think we can do something." He picked up the phone and called the kitchen. God knows what anybody was doing in the kitchen at that time of night, but he got a response, and about ten minutes later Kenni and I were noshing down on half a cold roast chicken, homemade bread, and Perrier. "There isn't a lot of room on the island for cows," Maxwell said apologetically. "We more or less do without milk. I had to learn to drink my coffee black."

I told him not to worry about it. "If you can stand to see a man talk with his mouth full, ask anything you want to know."

What he basically wanted to know was what the hell was going on here, thereby joining a rapidly growing club.

He wanted the whole story. I had already been through the whole thing for Buxton, but I wasn't bored going through it again. For one thing, Kenni was there to help me out and let me get chicken swallowed at intervals. For another thing, Maxwell was fun to watch.

He was trying to find out what he wanted to find out without letting on he was a DEA man. It was difficult for him, because he was a zealot. He was young, and handsome, and staunch, and ambitious, and he was stuck in a place the drug traffic had passed by. The DEA probably only maintained a presence here because of Gardeno, and the word was he was retired.

So I watched Maxwell dance all around the drug issue, trying to pretend he wouldn't rather have been in Colombia or Thailand, where you *knew* everyone you questioned was in the drug racket, instead of just having to hope they might be.

He said stuff like, "Mr. Schaeffer's behavior seems rather odd. Do you think he might have, you know, been *on* something?"

Or, "Did this Schaeffer, or the man who was murdered, what was his name?" As if he didn't have a good summary of everything Buxton knew already in his desk drawer.

"Watson Burkehart," Kenni supplied.

"Oh, yes. Did he ever mention the name Martin Gardeno?"

Kenni was about to blurt something, like the fact that *she* had mentioned him, but I got in first. "No," I said. "He never did. Why do you ask?"

He didn't want to tell me why he asked, which was fine with me. Then he said he'd have the car drive us to the ship, which was even better. I'd been watching Kenni out of the corner of my eye, and she was full of something besides chicken. She kept giving me significant looks, and looking at the clock and biting her lip.

So after we thanked Maxwell for the chicken, and he undoubtedly used code words while calling for the driver to have a tail put on us, and we were standing under the *porte cochere* waiting for the car with the flags, I muttered in Kenni's ear, "Hurry up and tell me what you want to tell me before you bust."

She leaned close to me and said, breathlessly, "There's been a message. From Schaeffer."

16

"Eeny meeny, chili beany. The spirits are about
to *speak!*"
—Bill Scott, "Rocky and His Friends" (syndicated)

"I found it stuck in your door jamb," Billy Palmer said. "I thought it
was a note meant for me, so I opened it."

"Why would I leave you a note?"

"We were supposed to talk about possible Network publicity when
we get back to New York."

He was right, we were. "Jeez, Bill, I'm sorry."

"Don't worry about it. You've had a lot on your mind."

"Everybody has. I've sort of lost touch with the tour. How's
everything going?"

"It's a mess, but the customers are loving it. Instead of wondering
who poisoned the egg, they won't talk about anything except what
could have happened to Schaeffer. Or rather, Ballantine, the character
we have him playing. Had him playing."

"You sound as exhausted as I feel."

"Worse. I just wish the passengers would stop finding this all so
fascinating."

"Wait till they go ashore later and see the headlines about
Burkehart's murder."

"Oh, God, is that going to be in the paper?"

"The first hot crime story in nearly thirty years? I think it's a safe
bet it will be in the paper."

Billy groaned. "I was telling Karen before that the hell of this is
that I would probably be eating this up, too, if I didn't have a hundred
paying customers to amuse. I mean, if I were on the ship as a regular
passenger and this stuff started happening, I'd probably have my
mouth watering to be in on it."

I held up the note—cream-colored S.S. *Caribbean Comet* stationery, which had come in a matching envelope. The envelope was blank. The notepaper had a few words of smeary, dot-and-dash handwriting, the kind you get from the pens they put in banks and hotel rooms.

I read the note again. No salutation or date.

"*You can play games, but sooner or later you'll have to talk to me. What's the matter, afraid I'll bite?*" It was signed "Lee."

I looked at Billy. "Did this thing make any sense to you?"

He thrust out his moustache and widened his eyes in a look of total bewilderment.

"To me?"

"It sure as hell doesn't make any to me. If I live a hundred years, I'll never call him Lee."

Billy nodded. "Come to think of it, he wanted us to call him Schafe. Mindy was the only one I know of who called him Lee."

"And she's not on the cruise. Unless she's here in disguise, of course."

Billy laughed. I didn't. He stopped.

"You're kidding, right?" he said.

"I don't know, Bill. I really don't." I shook my head. "You're sure this is his handwriting?"

"He's signed enough books for me. I mean, I'm not an expert, but I checked this against the inscription he wrote Saturday in my copy of *The Rotating Chasm*, and it looks the same to me. Karen, Kenni, and what's her name, the contest winner—"

"Jan Cullen."

"Yeah. They all think it looks the same."

"I suppose everybody handled the note."

"Well, yeah. Once I saw it was for you instead of me, I went looking for you. I found Kenni, who was just on her way back out to go to the U.S. Embassy. She was telling Jan to call the Marines if she didn't hear from her in an hour. So I asked them where you were and showed them the note. Then we went back to my cabin to compare handwriting." He shook his head sadly. "Damn," he said. "Fingerprints never occurred to me."

I told him not to worry about it, explaining that I had already messed up any prints there might have been in Schaeffer's cabin, so we'd have nothing to compare them with, anyway.

"I do want to get this to an expert, though. This note and your book."

"Where are you going to find an expert on St. David's Island?"

"I'm not even going to look. I'm going to go out to the airport and ship this air express to my people in New York. They'll find an expert."

"Well, uh, okay. But tell them to be very careful with the book."

"If they hurt it, I'll get you a new one."

"It's not that. It's—I know this sounds callous—but if Schaeffer is really dead . . ."

I grinned at him. "Your book is worth a lot of money. I understand. You're not a ghoul, just a collector."

"Sometimes it's a curse."

"I'll tell them to be extra careful."

"Thanks. I mean, I still hope he's okay, if for no other reason than I want to tell him off when we find him."

"If I find him first, I'll save him for you." I turned to go, then thought of something else. "What are you going to do about your other problem? How are you going to decide who wins the prize, if no one sticks to the mystery you came up with?"

He rolled his eyes. "Karen's working on that. I give up. I think that if anyone can explain what we made up, combined with what's really been happening, without resorting to space aliens, we should call that the correct solution and give them the prize."

I was only concerned with what had really happened, but I knew how he felt.

I called Buxton and Maxwell next morning and told them I was shipping something off the island from the airport, and they could examine it if they wanted. Would they mind if I brought it around for them to look at? I didn't want it to be delayed too long. They both said, oh, no, thanks, but they did it in different ways. Buxton asked, very straightforwardly, if it was something that could possibly help his murder investigation. I told him I didn't know, which was honest, and I told him what it was. He still had no jurisdiction over Schaeffer, and there was no evidence linking the missing writer to anything, so he let it go, asking me only to let him know if I turned anything up. I was starting to make plans to lure the guy back to New York with me. It's so nice to be trusted.

"Just one thing, Cobb. You're shipping this from the airport?"

"That's right."

"Don't get homesick and wander onto a plane."

"The boat leaves tomorrow, you know. Are you really going to show a hundred American tourists the hospitality of the Royal Constabulary?"

"I have," he said, "a whole day to decide what to do." The voice said that this was a man under a lot of pressure. The men behind the development of Island tourism were undoubtedly after him to do one of two things—arrest the killer immediately, as long as it was someone whose guilt would not be embarrassing and scare tourists away; or sweep the whole thing under the rug. They had already called off the meetings they'd been supposed to have with me.

I felt for him, but I was damned if I was going to miss another football game. I told him I'd keep him informed, and hung up.

Maxwell pissed me off. It's hard to sound phony-sweet with someone hammering in the background, but Maxwell managed it.

"Why, Mr. Cobb," he chided me. "We're here to *serve* American citizens, not ride herd on them. You're under no suspicion here. There's no *reason* to inspect your package."

"I don't mind," I said.

"We wouldn't dream of it."

Of course they wouldn't. It may be presumptuous of me, but it annoys me when people proceed on the assumption that I am an idiot. I knew that package was going to be searched, and he knew that package was going to be searched. I had given him the opportunity to be civilized about it, and he had tried to jerk me around. The only thing I had accomplished was to make sure they'd get the searching done and still get it to my New York people with the minimum of delay. Which, I suppose, was the best I could have hoped for.

I left Kenni in Spot's care, and vice versa, then left the ship. There was a different customs man on duty, and I managed to get out of the building without having guns pointed at me. I flagged down a taxi and told him to bring me to the airport, and step on it. And he did, too. At times, our speed approached a breathtaking twenty-six miles an hour.

As I expected, we had a tail. The car didn't have flags on the bumpers, but it might as well have. I had toyed with the idea of checking out one of the rental motorbikes at the stand by the pier and shaking any tail I might have, but I had decided against it, because I didn't feel like going native to the extent of dying in a motorbike accident. It would also have upset Mr. Maxwell, not a bad idea in itself, but making, no doubt, for a delay in the delivery of the handwriting samples.

I went to the airline desk and made the necessary arrangements. The package would be picked up in New York by Mr. Harris Brophy or Ms. Shirley Arnstein. They would have credentials, and would sign for the package. I handed over the Network credit card.

Then, I took out another card and made it to a phone. I raised two operators and my secretary, but I finally wound up talking to Harris Brophy.

"Hello, Harris," I said.

"Hello, Matt. How's the weather?"

"The weather," I said, "stinks. Hot and humid."

"Don't complain. It's cold and rainy in New York."

"I prefer cold and rainy. You're sitting at my desk, aren't you, Harris?"

"I am acting in your stead, Matt. Boss."

Harris was amazing. He was small and handsome and charming. He had been with the Network longer than I had, and was far better suited to Special Projects work, since he had no scruples and a vast capacity for amusement at the troubles of others. He had been offered the vice presidency of the department before they tricked me into taking it, and had turned it down, saying he had no desire for command. Nevertheless, Dracula couldn't make for native soil at daybreak faster than Harris zoomed in on my desk whenever I was out of town.

"Okay," I told him, "act in my stead on this," and I gave him a list of chores to do.

"Got it," he said. I knew he hadn't written them down. Harris never wrote anything down. The chores would get done.

"Care to tell me what this is all about?"

"Sure," I said. "As soon as I know."

Judy Ryerson found me in the ship's library.

"Bleak," I said. "Unless you're a historical romance fan. Otherwise it's bleak."

"Kenni told me I'd find you here. Though with everything that's been going on, I don't know how you expect to find time to read."

"That's a hell of a thing for a writer's wife to say." She gave me a wan smile in return. "That's the problem," I went on. "Too much has been happening. My mind is starting to race. The only thing that accomplishes is that it drives me nuts. A good book would distract me, but this library seems to be stocked exclusively with the kind of books that get left behind in staterooms."

"I didn't come here for a book. I came here to see you."

"Oh? What about?"

"I want you to talk to Mike. I'm afraid for him."

"What do you mean?"

"Mike has been depressed for a long time, Matt. He didn't write anything for two years—he had some of the Flagellator books ghosted. He drank too much. We had to put him in the hospital for a while."

"I didn't know."

"We kept it quiet. But he was getting better. He *was* better. We thought the cruise would be a good way to celebrate, to get back into society."

"He seems to be doing fine."

"Mostly he was. Schaeffer got him down, a little. They were really good friends in the old days. Mike doesn't say so, because he thinks it would sound like sour grapes, but he read and revised Schaeffer's first book. Practically did a second draft on it. He can't understand how he could have turned so cold to him."

"He must understand it," I said. "He explained it perfectly first night out."

"Oh, he can explain it," Judy said. "He just can't believe it. In his heart. Mike comes on tough and brash, you know, but he is a very sensitive man."

"Schaeffer hasn't been around for days."

"I said Schaeffer got him down *a little*. Something happened today that really set him off."

"What?"

Tears came from Judy's eyes. All at once, like a conjuring trick. "*He won't tell me!* That's why I'm so worried. It has to be something the policeman said, but I don't even know that for sure. Things are bad when he starts keeping secrets from me. He just sits in the bar and drinks gin, and when I ask him what's wrong, he just smiles sadly at me."

She took a deep breath through her nose, wiped a savage forearm across her eyes. "God *damn* it!" she said. "I *will* not cry. I'm not going through it again. I love him, Matt, and I'll do anything to help him, but I cannot go through it all again."

She didn't mean it. Or rather, she meant it, it just wasn't true. If she had to, she'd go through it again. She'd do it for Mike, because she loved him. I felt a little anger that a man with a wife so devoted could still find something to be depressed about.

"I'll talk to him," I said. "Anything you'd like me to say?"

"Just find out what's *bothering* him. Oh, try to get him away from the liquor if you can, but that's not as important."

"Sometimes, on a thing like this, the more the merrier."

She smiled through the wreckage the tears had made of her face. It was a grisly sight, but I admired her spirit.

"Phil DeGrave should already be there. He was easier to find than you were."

"He's got less on his mind. Listen, Judy, you go find somebody to talk to, too."

"Oh, Nicola and Mrs. Furst and Jan and Kenni have a regular kaffeeklatsch lined up. Instant support group. I think even Karen is taking some time out to be there, busy as she is."

"It's good to have friends."

"Ones who stick, at least. Unlike Mr. Schaeffer. I almost hope he *did* go overboard."

So she didn't know about the note. Kenni had said that she and Jan and Billy and Karen had decided to keep their mouths shut about it, but I wasn't expecting a whole lot. I'm a person who feels guilty keeping secrets. I can do it, but it takes a lot of effort. I never expect a secret to stay secret very long, so I'm always pleasantly surprised when it does.

I asked her if she wanted me to walk her to the coffee shop where the other women said they'd meet her, but she said she'd be fine, and shooed me along to see about her husband.

Mike Ryerson stared into a tall glass as if it were a crystal ball. "I should have slugged the bastard when I had the chance."

Phil DeGrave had the look on his face that teetotalers get when they try to converse with drunks. "You lost me. Which bastard, the cop? That's all you needed to do. How would Judy feel with you in some foreign clink?"

Mike lifted the glass to eye level and squinted at it. Apparently, he liked what he saw, because he lowered the drink and sucked at it the way a baby pulls at a bottle. He swallowed, then worked his lips a few times, as though reluctant to replace the liquor with words. He mumbled something.

Phil said, "What?"

"Not the cop, I said." Mike practically yelled it. "Not the cop, why the hell would I want to slug the cop? He was just doing his job. I should have slugged Burkehart, that bastard. The night he was giving the old lady a hard time about smoking."

Phil took a deep breath. I'd come to his rescue in a minute, but they hadn't seen me yet, and I was learning a lot.

Phil took another deep breath and tried logic, always a mistake with a drunk. "Mike," he said, "if what I hear is true, and from what the cops asked me, I gather it is, someone reduced Burkehart's head to the approximate shape of an ashtray. A slugging by you or anybody shortly before that seems superfluous."

Mike mumbled again. Phil heard it better than I did. He said, "What satisfaction would you have had?"

Mike took three big swallows from his drink. He had a mild smile on his face when he took the glass away. "The satisfaction," he said, "of having at least done *something* to that son of a bitch before I get accused of killing him."

Phil was on the verge of total exasperation. "Come *on*, Mike. For God's sake. They questioned everybody on the ship about Burkehart. They questioned everybody in the tour twice. Hell, they hauled Matt Cobb off at gunpoint to the police station last night!"

"That's right," I said. "They did."

I got two jaundiced looks, one drunk, one sober.

"How long have you been there?" Phil demanded. I've found that writers do a lot of eavesdropping, but they hate to be eavesdropped upon.

I lied cheerfully. "Just this second," I said, then deflected further comment by flagging the bartender and ordering a bourbon on the rocks.

"The only good part about being hauled off to the station is that they let me sleep through this morning's inquisition. Who was it, Buxton?"

"Is he the white guy?" Phil asked.

I laughed. "No, he just looks that way. I wouldn't mention it to him, either. He's very touchy about it, and he's likely to give you a tough time." My drink came. I paid, tipped, took a sip. I like a glass of bourbon now and then, but this one was more of a gesture of solidarity with Mike than anything else. "Or did he already give you a tough time?"

Phil raised his eyebrows. "Me? No. Mike here thinks they're going to accuse him of murder."

I looked at Mike. "Really," I said. "Not just because you didn't like him. If they were arresting people for not liking Burkehart, I would be breaking chunks of guano on the Davidian chain gang already."

"Not just because I didn't like him," Mike said. "Because I saw him. In town, ashore. I had an argument with him."

"Oh, boy," Phil said.

"And I lied to the cops about it." Mike drained his glass, angrily, as though he were teaching it a lesson. He slammed it down on the bar. "And they caught me at it."

17

"If you can't get to the game, get to a phone."
—George Steinbrenner, Dial It/SportsPhone commercial

I looked at him. I saw one encouraging sign. His glass was empty, and he was looking around for the bartender.

"Tell us about it," I suggested.

"Might as well. It will be in all the papers when they arrest me."

"Come on," Phil said. "If it was as bad as all that, they'd have arrested you already. The ship sails tomorrow."

Please God and Inspector Buxton, I added silently. Still, Phil had a point. Mike saw it and looked vaguely encouraged.

"I was hitting bookstores in Davidstown. They've only got two or three, you know. One of them had Nicola's latest book, Phil. None of yours, or mine. I found the new Dick Francis, though. British edition. Won't be out in the States for another six months.

"Anyway, when I finished that, I was thirsty. You'd think an island this hot, more of the shops would be air-conditioned."

"They are," I said.

"They are?"

"Sure. It's just that the Islanders' idea of cool starts at a higher temperature."

"Sure," Phil echoed. "Outside it's ninety-five, inside it's eighty-eight, they think they're cool."

Mike smiled. "Suggestible bunch, aren't they?" He gave a little chuckle. "Maybe they do it to help their saloon trade. I went looking for one when I got tired of looking in bookstores."

"Judy wasn't with you," I said.

"No, dammit. She would have kept me out of this mess." He

shook his head. "I don't think I'll ever leave her sight again. If I stay out of jail. If she still wants me."

He took time for a big sigh, then went on. "It was dark in the bar, but I saw him right away. He was in a booth in the back. He wasn't making himself conspicuous, but he wasn't hiding, either. It was just after opening, and there were about three other people in the bar besides the two of us.

"He spoke first. He looked up at me, kind of surprised, and said, 'Are you the errand boy?'"

"Whose errand boy?" I asked.

Mike scratched an eyebrow. "That's what I wanted to know. When I asked him, he wasn't talking. He gave me a disgusted look and said he only wanted to deal with principals."

I held up a hand. "Hold it. Principals A-L-S, or principles L-E-S?"

Mike shrugged. "I assumed the first way. I don't think Burkehart had much in the way of L-E-S principles."

"Then what happened?"

"I started razzing him."

"Not smart," Phil DeGrave said. "For all you knew the other people in the bar were friends of his, with knives."

"According to the cop," Mike said dolefully, "they couldn't give two shits about him, but they all had memories like elephants. They remembered me, they remembered I accused him of being a thief, they remembered I didn't like him. They said I threatened him, but that wasn't true. I just said what I said a little while ago—I should have hit him when I had the chance."

Mike looked down at the bar. "Don't I have a drink somewhere?"

"What happened then?" I asked. Better to keep him talking. From the looks of things, he'd pass out at his next drink, anyway.

"Wha? Oh, next. Next I told him I was gonna tell the captain where he was, and I left the bar. I guess *that* was a threat, wasn't it? But it wasn't the kind of threat that winds a guy up *dead* later, was it?"

"Of course not," I said.

"Phil. Phil, you're a writer. Nobody would be justified in taking it that way, right?"

"Like Matt said, of course not."

"Good. Good. You both testify for me."

"But you didn't tell the captain."

Mike squinted at me through bleary eyes. He was on the way out. "Tell him what?"

"Where Burkehart was."

"Nah. The captain's a Swede. I hate Swedes. They talk funny."

"Actually," Phil said, "he's a Norwegian."

Mike grinned at me. "Phil's a nice guy, but he's a pedantic bastard, you ever notice that?" He turned his head. It wobbled like a bobbing-head doll. "You're a pedantic bastard, Phil."

The head wobbled back to me. "Anyway, who cared where Burkehart was? I was glad he was off the ship. If I told the captain, he'd probably have had the bastard hauled back in irons, or something, a tight-assed Swede like him. I hate Swedes. They talk funny, and they're sticklers for rules. And they pretend to be Norwegians."

"So why'd you lie to the cops?" I asked.

"Thought it would be less complicated if I didn't let anyone know I'd had an argument with the guy a few hours before someone flattened his face, that's all. Didn't want to get involved."

"That wasn't smart, Mike," Phil said. He *was* pedantic sometimes. "You've written enough mysteries to know the cops always find out, and things always look worse after they do."

"Wasn't thinking about mysteries," Mike said. "I was thinking about the men's adventures I've done. The Flagellator always gets away with lying to the cops." He laughed, loud and sharp like a blast from a trombone. Then he looked at the bar again, felt around it with his hands. "What did I do with that goddam drink?"

"I'm going to change the subject, Mike. I mention this because that's something you should never spring on a drunk unexpectedly."

Mike nodded gravely. "Good point."

"Who called Schaeffer Lee?"

"Not me. Not macho enough for him. I called him Schafe, when I didn't call him Hiram."

"Hiram?"

"That's what the *H* stands for. Made me promise never to tell anyone, and I never did until now. You devious bastard, you get me drunk and you make me break a solemn vow. Ah, the hell with him. Treated me like a leper, anyway."

"So nobody but Mindy ever called him Lee."

"Who the hell is Mindy?"

"Up until just before we sailed, his girlfriend."

Mike shrugged. "Yeah, yeah. Girls called him Lee. He had all these different codes, you know, ways he had worked out to act with different people. That's his trouble. The son of a bitch is so busy acting some way, he doesn't leave himself any time to *be* anything."

Mike brightened. "Hey, that's good. Isn't it? Phil, remind me of that when I'm sober, I'll use it in a book. I'm a hell of a writer, ain't I?"

Now, I decided, was the time. "Judy's worried about you, Mike."

He started to cry. First Schaeffer and now him. Billy and Karen could advertise. "Take our cruises and see Matt Cobb reduce grown men to tears."

"Poor Judy," Mike sobbed. "I put her through so much. I'm such an asshole, and she loves me anyway. She's way too good for me, Matt, she is. She'd be better off without me."

"She doesn't think so," I said.

Mike sneered at me. "Ah, you're a bachelor, what the hell do you know?" He turned to Phil. "Judy's way too good for me, Phil."

Phil shrugged. "Nicola's too good for me, too. If women like Judy and Nicola waited around for men who were good enough for them, the human race would have died out long ago."

"Phil, Phil, Phil. You bullshit artist. Even drunk I can see that doesn't make any sense." He laughed again.

"The sentiment is clear," Phil said. He sounded a little defensive. Writers don't like it when you accuse them of bullshit. "I'll work on it."

"Before you do," I said, "help me take him back to Judy."

I walked back to my stateroom with a warm feeling of accomplishment, my first since that Ping-Pong game, which seemed to have taken place sometime back in the Mesozoic era.

There was a note on my door. S.S. *Caribbean Comet* envelope.

I reached for it eagerly. Maybe it was another message from "Lee." I could hardly wait to read what he had to say.

Another disappointment. It wasn't from Lee, it was from the ship's switchboard operator. There had been a phone call for me from Mr.

Harris Brophy in New York, and he would wait at the office until he heard from me. The note had been taken down just after I left the last time, so Harris hadn't had too long to wait.

I went inside, picked up the phone, and asked the operator if I could call New York from here. She said sure, when the boat was docked, it plugged into the Davidstown phone system, but that I could only make collect or credit-card calls. I said that was fine with me, whipped out my credit card, and set the gears in motion.

It took ten minutes for the call to go through. I used the time to look at the ceiling and think. It was a very nice ceiling, for a ship. The thinking yielded only a question. Why is there a nautical term for every goddam part of a ship except ceilings? Maybe there was and I just didn't know it. Like the explanations for all the crazy things that had been going on, and this is where I came in.

I was about to call the operator back and accuse her of making me frustrated by giving me too much time to think, but she got to me first.

"Your New York call, Mr. Cobb."

"Matt?"

"Yeah, Harris. Why didn't you have them page me?" I asked. "It would have made me feel important."

"Oh, is that all it takes?"

"I'm easy to please."

"I'll remember that. I didn't have them page you because I thought you might want the opportunity to get to a secure phone."

"You found something hot?"

"How do I know what's hot? I don't have the slightest idea what's going on there."

"Welcome to the club."

Harris went on as if he hadn't heard me. "You asked me to check something, I got it checked. Also, there's been a bit of news, possibly."

"Is it something I might be more pleased that the police not know?"

"You mean the police where you are? I don't see how, but as I say, I don't know the situation."

"Then go ahead and tell me. We're all friends down here."

"Some friend or other opened your package before it got here, you know."

I smiled. "Just as long as it got there on time."

"No problem, there Got here quicker than I expected, in fact."

"The Consular Service is there to help American citizens in every way possible "

"Some day, you must take a few hours and explain this all to me Like why you're cackling like a chicken at this moment."

"Just a small triumph, Harris. I'll explain it after I get back. It would be too depressing to go into now. What's the scoop?"

"The note is the real thing, according to Dr. Smendlon. There's a lot of technical stuff—weight, ascenders, descenders, bowls, but what it boils down to is that the hand that wrote the inscription is the hand that wrote the note."

"That was the consensus," I said.

"That's nice," Harris said.

"So, either I've got a forger who's too good for Dr. Smendlon, or he's still alive, right? Alive and around. That was ship's stationery, after all. Unless, of course, someone has been planning this since long before the cruise and got hold of the stationery ahead of time."

Harris snorted. "And got Schaeffer to oblige him by writing the note ahead of time? Then got Schaeffer to further oblige him by allowing himself to be murdered or hidden or both?"

"I thought you didn't know anything about this?"

"Come on, boss." He knows I hate it when he calls me boss. "The name was in the book; you're on the other end talking about being 'alive or around.' It doesn't take Jessica Fletcher to deduce what you're talking about."

"Still," I said, "it's possible."

"It's possible there's a mental hospital on that island, and it's possible you ought to check into it. Is Schaeffer really missing? Possibly dead?"

"That's only part of it, but it's accurate as far as it goes."

"You ought to find him."

"Thank you, Harris."

"Don't mention it."

"*I've done practically nothing but look for the son of a bitch since Sunday morning!*" I said. "Aside from chasing some missing cutlery and getting involved in a murder case."

"A different murder case?"

"As far as I can tell," I said cautiously, "a different murder case."

"You're okay to work for, Matt," Harris said, "but the assignments you give out aren't half as interesting as the ones you keep for yourself."

"Mr. Greedy," I said. "Why are you so hot to have me find Schaeffer? One of his legion of fans?"

"No, just a loyal employee. Schaeffer's a big moneymaker for the Network."

"But 'They Call Me Shears' isn't on our Network."

"But the Stephen Shears books are published by Austin, Stoddard & Trapp."

I said, "Ah." Austin, Stoddard, and Trapp were all dead. Their publishing company was now a wholly owned subsidiary of the Network.

"That makes my day, Harris." I made a note to pay more attention to whom AS&T was publishing.

"I thought it would."

"You said you had some news."

"The cops think they've found Joe Jenkins."

They say a cruise ship is a world of its own. I believed it, now. I had been so wrapped up in what had happened since we left New York, I had completely forgotten the missing disk jockey.

"What do you mean, they think they've found him?"

"Well, his remains, more accurately."

"Ah," I said again.

"Some humanitarian left him out to be food for urban wildlife in a drainpipe in Riverside Park. Rain kept him soft. He was pretty ripe by the time the Parks Department got around to investigating all the complaints they've had about the smell."

"When was this?"

"Yesterday."

"He's been missing since goddam September!"

"Come on, Matt. Can you blame the Parks Department people for not putting a class-A priority on a smelly drain in New York? At the end of the summer?"

"You have a point."

"Thank you. Anyway, the reason nobody's *absolutely* sure it's Jenkins is that while the rats and cats and whatever left some skin on his fingers, there was only enough to get a partial print off one thumb Jenkins had been arrested once or twice for coke, you knew that, so there was something to compare it with, but the experts could only match seven points, and you need ten for positive ID "

"So why don't they do dental work?"

"There was no dental work His head was smashed into more pieces than a stepped-on cannoli "

18

"When you care enough to send the very best."
                              —Hallmark Cards commercial

"Hmmm," I said. "I don't suppose, Harris, that the big blow happened to be a shot upward to the base of the skull?"

"I like the way you assume I've had a look at the autopsy reports."

"I'd be disappointed in you if you hadn't." Harris would have made a terrific gossip columnist. His curiosity was insatiable, and his sources were fantastic. He specialized in secretaries. I used to think he used sex appeal, but it goes too far for that. Elderly schoolteacher types, men, the plain and the pimply, he had them all willing to tell him things. If it sits behind a desk and knows something, Harris can get what ever he wants. He says he just asks, and they tell him because he has an honest face.

"How did you know about the shot to the occipital? Lucky guess?"

"Then there was one," I said.

"Yeah. Ask that question in the hearing of the right police officers, and you could be in for an interesting time."

I grunted. "I'm already having an interesting time."

"I've noticed."

"Anything else of interest in the report?"

"Just that all the teeth were smashed."

"On purpose, to delay identification? Or just a lucky shot on the killer's part?"

"Oh, definitely on purpose. Four or five of the shots were devoted to smashing up the teeth. Oh, and they found the murder weapon."

"Somehow, I don't think it was a custom-made, monogrammed golf club."

"No, it was a nice, anonymous chunk of gray limestone. The killer left it right near the body."

"Jolly. Anything else?"

"No, that's about it. Unless, of course, the cops are holding on to something to check phony confessions against. They have ways of keeping that sort of thing out of reports that might leak."

"How's the Network?"

"Girding up for the November sweeps. Routine, otherwise. The biggest thrill here at Special Projects is a nut who is threatening the Network with dire things because we, quote, 'won't let any smart people be on game shows,' unquote. This persons knows it's a conspiracy, because he or she has tried out for all of them, and been turned down every time. I've got the West Coast office working on it."

Gosh, I thought. Nut letters. Routine. It made me damn near homesick.

The current situation, on the other hand, just made me sick.

I bit my lip, thinking. Finally I said, "Harris, I'm going to dictate a full report on this cruise and send it to you. Listen to it, have a good laugh. If you think of anything, let me know. If anything happens to me, follow up on it."

"What's going to happen to you?"

"Probably nothing, but what's life if you don't play a long shot now and then?"

I expected some wiseass remark from Harris, but I didn't get one. He just said okay and told me to be careful. Maybe he *did* like me. Talk about long shots. The smart money, looking at Harris, would say he didn't like anybody.

I said good-bye, put the phone back on the hook, and stood there, thinking.

Joe Jenkins was dead. Joe Jenkins had been murdered. Joe Jenkins had been murdered, weeks ago, in precisely the way Watson Burkehart had been murdered yesterday. What was the connection?

I was the connection. One connection, anyway. I had been supervising the search for Jenkins back in New York, and I had been working Burkehart to find out what had happened to Lee H. Schaeffer. And I was tied in with Schaeffer, too, if only in short-lived, but sincere, mutual dislike.

"I've got it!" I said brightly. Spot looked up at me expectantly. "*I'm* the killer!"

Spot put his head back down. I guessed it wouldn't work, at that. Still, it would be a nice twisty ending. The kind Billy and Karen liked to provide for their guests.

All of a sudden, though, I looked more and more important to this case in ways I couldn't understand. The one concrete result of Joe Jenkins's disappearance had been that I replaced him on this cruise. The question presented itself: Was Joe Jenkins offed for the *express purpose* of getting me on the goddam boat?

How could someone even arrange something like that? I missed Kenni. She was good at this stuff. It was hard to keep doing the questions and answers all by myself. I wondered where she was— with Mike returned and contrite, Judy wouldn't need the moral support anymore.

I told myself to stop it. Kenni didn't have to answer to me for her whereabouts. Maybe she'd met some millionaire mystery collector who was sweeping her off her feet with offers to buy her her own library. I'd be happy for her, I lied to myself.

To hell with it. She'd turn up when she turned up.

The answer to my last question, then. It wouldn't, in fact, have been hard for someone to arrange. Provided, of course, the person knew enough about me to know that contest had been more or less my idea, and enough about Marv Bachman to know that he was exactly the kind of pain in the ass who would wish the assignment on me for that very fact. A little iffy, perhaps, to commit murder on the strength of, but hell, that's just a sane person's logic. People who are willing to commit murder have a logic all their own.

I tried to think of a few candidates, but short of Harris, which was ridiculous, I drew a blank. Then I tried to think of something, anything, that would tie this scenario with Schaeffer, Burkehart, or both, and came up with a blank in three dimensions; a void.

There was *no motive*. It was driving me crazy. As far as I could tell, there was *no motive* for *anybody* to have done *anything*.

No. I take it back. Burkehart might have stolen the knives to sell them for money. That was the kind of good, wholesome motive anybody could understand. Clem, the chef, had said they were Swiss-forged, a complete set of top-quality butcher's tools. That could fetch a good price.

Fine. So where the hell were they? They weren't on the ship, unless, of course, Schaeffer had hidden them. Maybe I should wait for another note.

Spot lifted his head and looked at the door. I said, "Come in," just before the knock. Jan and Kenni walked in, looking impressed.

"And Burkehart didn't swim ashore with them tied around his neck, either," I said.

Kenni came over and gave me a kiss on the forehead. "What are you talking about?" she asked pleasantly.

Jan looked at me with a certain amount of hostility. "How did you do that?" she demanded.

"Do what?"

"Say come in just before I knocked? I know we didn't make any noise." She pointed at her feet and Kenni's. They both wore tennis shoes. "And we didn't do any talking, because we're all talked out."

"My God," Kenni said. "I'm all for support groups, women together and all that, but you'd think these things could end when the woman you're supporting gets her problem solved. I wanted to leave, but somehow, it didn't seem polite."

"It wouldn't have been," Jan said. "But it's beside the point. How did you know we were out there?"

"Can't you figure it out?"

"I hate being mystified! I should have just let Kenni say she was me, and skipped this trip altogether."

I had to blink a few times before I believed my eyes. Jan, the previously imperturbable, was really upset. And not about a little mystification, either. I'd have to ask Kenni about it later.

"Come on, Matt," Jan said. "Stop wasting time. You didn't see us. You didn't hear us."

I looked at her, not knowing what to say. It was incredible, how upset she was.

Finally, I turned to Kenni and said, "Tell her how I knew."

Kenni didn't smile. She was apparently walking softly around Jan this afternoon. "Spot probably did something, Jan. We were too quiet for Matt, but not for the dog."

Spot got to his feet, as if to take a bow.

Jan grumbled.

Kenni said, "Now you can answer my question. What was that about Burkehart?"

So I went through the whole thing again, this time with Kenni. Her only contribution, besides companionship, was, "Why is this Harris character ridiculous?"

"Because he was in New York, doing my job. He wasn't in Davidstown killing somebody he never met."

"He could have hired somebody. Or he could have made himself scarce for the afternoon. It's what? A two hour plane ride from New York?"

I looked at her. She was right, as far as that went. I'd come to St. David's Island on a ship, and I'd been more or less assuming that that was how you got here. Stupid. Unless you are neurotic, and refuse to fly, nobody takes a ship to *get* anywhere. You take a ship because you want to be on a ship. It would be perfectly possible, weather and schedules permitting, to fly here from New York, kill Burkehart, and fly back in less than half a day.

"But that would mean Burkehart and Jenkins had no connection with what's happened on the ship."

"So?" Kenni asked. Another stumper.

"Can you think of a motive for this man to have done all this? Killed Jenkins, sent me to sea, zoomed down here to kill Burkehart?"

"Maybe he wants your job," Jan suggested. She'd been sitting in the corner, sulking and morose, giving Spot a desultory pet every now and then. We'd almost forgotten she was there.

Her eyes flashed impatiently when we looked at her. "Or maybe he just wants to make you look bad. Don't look at me like that. Lee Schaeffer was jealous of you, why shouldn't somebody who works for you be, too?"

"In the abstract, no reason, granted I'm somebody to be envious of. But in this specific case, Harris could have my job in the first place. And I've been offering it to him ever since. Also, he constantly makes me look bad."

Kenni was at the desk, resting her face on her fist, tapping with the leaky room pen. She looked as miserable as Jan.

"So what are we going to do now?" she asked.

Good question. I thought it over for a second, and realized that what I'd been doing here for the past hour was avoiding the decision my unconscious mind had reached long ago.

"Well, *I* am going to follow a principle that has served me in good stead over the years."

"What's that?" Kenni wanted to know.

"If you're not getting anywhere being smart, do something stupid."

"Such as what?" Jan asked.

"I am going to go try to pay a call on Martin Gardeno. *He's* been driving me crazy."

"But he hasn't done *anything*!" Kenni said.

"Precisely. And it bothers me. A big-time criminal, living on a small island, who has nothing whatever to do with a series of mysterious events. It's as unsatisfying in its way as the knives nobody's been cut with. So I think I'll go out there and ask him why not."

"Count me in," Kenni said cheerfully.

Jan went off like a bomb.

"*Games!* You people can never get away from *games*! Are you both *crazy*? This Gardeno was a Mafia boss. A killer. You might as well ask him to murder you. You make me sick! You're both going to *die*!"

19

"And see this living legend's *fabulous* home!"
—Robin Leach, "Lifestyles of the Rich and Famous"
(syndicated)

"Mr. Gardeno will see you in a moment." The butler bowed and retreated. Seeing this guy was worth the entire trip. He was old, his hands were pink-spotted and deformed with arthritis, but he stood ramrod straight and his voice was strong and smooth. I had expected to be frisked; I had expected Kenni's bag to be searched. I hadn't expected to be welcomed with the kind of sober politeness even the British have forgotten about.

Kenni and I were seated in a room paneled in dark wood. There was an ornate and perfectly superfluous marble fireplace on the far wall. The chairs we sat on were covered in silk striped purple and gold, matching the curtains on the windows. Past the curtains, we could see the sun beating down on palm trees, and, way down the hill, on the white balconies of the new hotel. It was like an unwelcome message from the Twentieth Century.

I looked around at crystal and silver and porcelain. "Crime does not pay," I said.

Kenni said, "What?"

"Never mind. What were you thinking about?"

"If the butler would smile, he would look just like Uncle Ben."

"So glad I asked."

Kenni shrugged. "Well, what were you thinking about?"

"The ways in which the money to buy this beautiful place was earned."

Kenni looked severe. "Matt!" she whispered. "What if the place is bugged?"

"What if it is? I don't think I'm surprising anybody. If you're nervous, you should have stayed back on the ship with Jan."

"I hope I never get that nervous. What's got into her?"

I smiled. "I was going to ask you the same thing. If you don't know of any concrete reason, my guess is confusion overload."

"You say that as if it's a recognized medical condition."

"Only by me. It happens all the time; not being able to do anything because it's impossible to tell what the right thing to do is. Makes me crazy."

"Is that why we're here? Because you went crazy?"

"That's why *I'm* here. You're here because you insisted. Also because you've already researched the guy and the island, and you might think of something I don't know."

"I'm indispensable," she said.

"Don't look so smug. I don't think we're in any danger, but I've been wrong before."

"I don't believe it."

"At least once or twice. Amazing, but true."

"The thing that amazes me," she said, suddenly serious, "is that we got past the gate at all. That guard with the mashed nose—I thought he was going to get nasty."

"He wasn't going to get nasty," I said, though I wasn't at all sure of that. It's somewhat disconcerting discovering a face that should be decorating a Brooklyn bookie joint in the middle of a tropical forest. "All he had to do to keep us out was keep the gate locked until we got sick of talking to him. Then what could we do? Turn around and bring the car back to the Avis office."

"That would have been disappointing."

"Especially after driving mountain roads at twenty miles an hour with my chin getting rubbed raw on the steering wheel. We should have borrowed the Cadillac from the Embassy."

"We would have gotten more respect from the guard."

"We *never* would have gotten in. Gardeno didn't hole up on this island to entertain American officials. Just the opposite."

"Everything changed when you handed the guy your card."

That had done it, all right. I had been working on my "do something stupid" principle. I'd already given my name a hundred times, said I had nothing to do with the governments of the United States or St. David's Island, and just if I could make an *appointment* to see Mr. Gardeno some time today or early tomorrow morning. Nothing. So I contorted myself in the compact car (the guard had sort of growled every time I got close to the door handle), reached my card case and a pen, scribbled the ship's number on the card, and handed it to the guard. "In case he changes his mind," I said as I handed it to him, knowing even as I did so that the odds were overwhelmingly in favor of the card becoming part of the talus on the floor of the forest before we were even out of sight.

The Brooklyn Boy looked at the card and his face lit up as though it had a thought behind it. He said we should wait, then went back into his little air-conditioned cabin and picked up a phone.

I'm not a great lip-reader, but I'm okay. I know he spoke the words "Boss" and "Network" several times, and I thought I picked out "Let him know" near the end.

Finally, he popped out of the booth, leaned down (way down) to the car window, and said, "Okay. You can go in. I'm taking a chance. If you make me look bad, I'll get real upset. I don't have to stay on this island, you know. Times are, I'd be glad to be deported. Understand me?"

The honest answer to that was "Huh?" but I was being polite. I just told him we wouldn't dream of making him look bad, and drove through the gate before he changed his mind.

So here we were. I didn't know about Kenni, but I was irritated. I'd come here to try to get some answers, and all I'd gotten was more stuff that didn't make sense.

I kept telling myself we were perfectly safe. Jan was our life insurance. Gardeno had to keep his nose perfectly clean on St. David's Island. The government was dying for an excuse to deport him, and back in the States, the Justice Department drooled at the thought of getting their hands on him. If anything happened to us, if we disappeared, for example, Jan could go to Buxton and swear out a statement that Kenni and I had intended to, and had taken steps toward, visiting Martin Gardeno. That would be enough for Buxton to come down on this place like a ton of guano. Gardeno didn't want that kind of trouble.

I kept telling myself all that. When I found myself insisting on it to myself with growing anger at myself for not entirely believing it, I started looking around for something else to think about.

It wasn't necessary. The butler came in, showed us another little bow, and said, "Mr. Gardeno will see you now."

The butler led us down a hall and into a room. We stepped from Edwardian England to Italian Brooklyn before we could blink. The room was filled with television sets and junk. There were five sets, all color, all expensive, on a specially built set of shelves. Every set was on, each to a different channel. Facing the set was an enormous green leather reclining chair. The back of it was big enough to show movies on. Either the chair was on fire, or its still-invisible occupant was smoking an especially foul cigar. Blue-gray smoke curled up from the chair and became part of the general haze that filled the top third of the room, impervious to the best efforts of an expensive air-conditioning system.

Except for the heavily curtained window, the whole room was shelves. Shelves filled with bowling and fishing and softball trophies, with plaster Cupids and plaster Virgin Marys, with pictures of dark-eyed little girls in white dresses looking sweet, or of dark-eyed little boys with wise-guy smiles on their faces.

The butler said, "Miss Clayton and Mr. Cobb, sir."

There was a wheezing from the chair that sounded like a jeep failing to start. A wrinkled claw of a hand reached down to the floor and picked up a paper bag that had been sitting there. Its top had been neatly cuffed two inches to give it stability. The bag disappeared behind the chair. The wheezing became a rasp, then a loud wet explosion. A voice that was something between a whisper and a gag said, "Goddam."

The bag went back down to the floor. The hand waved feebly, as though blown by a breeze. "Come here," the voice said. "Sit where I can see you."

Kenni gave me a what-did-you-get-me-into look, which was hardly fair. I shrugged. I walked forward and got my first look at Martin Gardeno.

The man the New York papers had liked to call The Big Boss or The Strongman was a *shrimp*, and an old, frail, crippled one at that. He leaned back in the recliner as if he were too weak to lift his head. His hair was yellow-white, and uncombed, so it looked as if it had been pasted randomly to his skull. He wore thick glasses. They magnified his eyes so much, all you could see through the glass was liquid brown. Forget lenses like Coke-bottle bottoms, these looked like entire bottles of Coke.

He wore a red plaid shirt, open to show a wrinkled neck, heavy gray corduroy pants, white socks, and slippers. He could have bought it all at the boys' department at Sears. The pants, thick though they were, weren't heavy enough to disguise the fact that he wore heavy braces on both legs. The legs never moved.

He smiled at us, showing big, even teeth a shade darker than the hair. The brown liquid sloshed around in the spectacles.

"Welcome," he said. "Welcome, welcome." He raised his right hand, put a twisted black cigar in his mouth, then stuck the hand out to me. It took me a second to realize he was offering to shake hands. The hand didn't tremble with the delay, it just started to sink, as though his muscles had become bored with his orders.

I hadn't come here to make an old man lose face. I caught the hand before it had sunk too far. Willpower gave him a fraction of a second of a respectable grip, and I let him go as soon as it was ended.

"Sit down," he said again. He gestured toward a chair to the left of the bank of TV sets. Kenni was already seated in an identical one on the other side.

"I get so few visitors from the States," he said. "An old man gets homesick." His smile could have been anything from an effort to ingratiate himself, to the wicked amusement of a cat with a mouse.

Sitting where I was, I had lost his eyes completely. Now, instead of the brown liquid, I got a kaleidoscope of TV images. Here a commercial, here a soap opera, here a game show.

"I just sit here and watch the tube. The tubes. But I hate to miss anything. Cost me a fortune to have the satellite dish put up, but I had to do it. You know St. David's Island gets only *one channel*?" He shook his head; the TV reflections danced. "Then Haskins got all mopey that the dish ruined the look of the place, so I had to pay some English architect to put a ritzy-looking shack over the goddam thing—excuse me, Miss—that wouldn't interfere with the signals. Cost me—"

He reached for the bag, wheezed, coughed and spat, said "goddam" and put the bag back down. This time he didn't apologize to Kenni. He probably went through the routine so often he no longer noticed the curse was part of the routine.

"Cost me *another* fortune, but what are you gonna do?"

"Haskins is the butler?" Kenni asked.

He grinned again. "Yeah. Ain't he something? He came with the house. The Englishman I bought this place from wouldn't sell it to me unless I promised to let Haskins live here forever. I figured why not, he's as old as I am, how long can he last? And besides, the Englishman told me Haskins had been living and working here since he was ten years old. So I fixed him up a nice apartment and everything, and told him he could retire, but he don't trust nobody to look after the place but him. So he gets up every day and puts on the monkey suit and does what he's always done."

"He does nice work," I said. "All by himself?"

"Nah. He's got relatives and stuff come in, and my boys help. Runs them all like a sergeant, Haskins does. Everywhere but this room. This room is mine. Haskins hates it, keeps after me to let him 'fix it up' a little, but no way."

Wheeze. Cough. Spit. Another puff on the cigar.

"So I buy this huge estate, and I live like I got a one-room apartment in New York, like when I first moved out of my old man's house. Life, huh?"

He turned a little and his left eye came clear of the TV reflections. The circle of brown had become a thick line.

"Tell you why I let you in," he said.

"I'd like to know that," I admitted.

"Oh, I ain't being a bad host, by the way. Any minute now, Haskins will be here—"

And there he was with a drink cart. If I'd asked for absinthe or slivovitz or anything, Haskins could have produced it. I disappointed the hell out of him by taking only a Perrier with assorted citrus fruits. Kenni got more into the spirit of things and asked for a St. David's Island rum and Coke.

So now we were sociable. Gardeno picked up where he left off.

"Why I let you in. It was your card. Three things. First, that you worked for the Network in New York. Live in the city?"

We told him we did, so we had twenty minutes of New York politics. Gardeno missed talking New York City politics, was up on it better than I was—his satellite brought him hours of New York local news, and he never missed a minute of it.

"This corruption makes me sick," he said at one point, punctuating the sentence by depositing an especially large gob into the paper bag.

"Don't tell me you never bribed an official," Kenni said, protective of the city as only an immigrant can be. As soon as she said it, she sat back and effaced herself, remembering no doubt who she was talking to.

There was nothing to worry about. Gardeno threw back his head and treated us to the sight of his scrawny neck. He laughed until he choked. He choked for a long time. I sat there watching him, thinking I do *not* wish to give this disgusting old man mouth-to-mouth resuscitation. On the other hand, I didn't want to have to explain to the guy at the gate how Mr. Gardeno happened to choke to death while I was watching him.

But Gardeno saved himself, this time. He beat himself on the chest, cleared his throat with a sound like a chain saw starting up, and grinned at Kenni.

Gardeno wheezed a few more times, then said, "Yes, Miss, I did my share of that. In my illegal days. I don't do any of that stuff no more, ask anybody. Ask the Minister of Justice of this whole island if Martin Gardeno is clean or what. But you know what makes for corruption? Do you?"

Kenni didn't like the old man, and she was having a hard time hiding it. I hoped his vision was as bad as the glasses made it seem. Prodded, she said, "Tell me."

"Too many god—goddarned laws, Miss. I'm not talking about the laws guys like me used to mess around with. I'm talking about the nuisance laws a legit businessman has to find his way around or else starve to death. You give some bureaucrat, some Civil Service grade who don't have to worry about the bottom line, or if he does, it's just how do we stick the taxpayer for it—you give a guy like that the power of life or death over an honest businessman, it don't take no Amazing Kreskin to see what's gonna happen. The honest businessmen are gonna disappear—either they get smart and pay bribes, or they get driven from business. The crooked bureaucrats—enough of them to make the whole city stink—get rich. And the city gets a notch closer to being taken over by those slick, collegewise bastids— excuse me, Miss—who run the outfit now."

It was an incredibly clear and accurate analysis. I felt that way because I had made myself unpopular at countless New York City cocktail parties outlining the same thesis. Lots of civil servants go to cocktail parties.

Kenni, who (I had almost forgotten) worked for the city, and, come to think about it, had at least some power to affect the livelihood of every mystery writer alive, was getting huffy.

"I would think you'd approve of that."

Gardeno was aghast. "The outfit taking over the city? It would be a *catastrophe*."

"Well," Kenni said. "The honest citizens would certainly feel that way—"

"Fu—the *heck* with the honest citizens, Miss. It would be a catastrophe for the *outfit*. Look at what's happening now. You get too cozy with the power structure, you're too easy to find. That wop Giuliani is having a field day."

Gardeno leaned forward and spoke confidentially. "You know, since I been on this godforsaken sweatbox of an island, I've had a lot of time to think. And I come to realize, when the outfit controls too much, things go to hell. I mean, outfit guys got to live in the city, too. You may sell all the dope in the world, and be rich as anything, but some Puerto Rican crackhead isn't going to check for credentials before he sticks a shiv in your daughter's ribs so he can grab her purse to buy some more dope from you. It's, what do you call it, it's a paradox, but crime chokes itself if it takes over too much of a place. It takes honest citizens to make money. Crime can only steal it. Vegas would have died out long ago if honest people from all over didn't come to lose their money. Not that everybody in Vegas is crooked, but they sure don't *make* anything out there but their percentage. Percentage of *what* is what the straight world is all about.

"You take a place like Chicago in the twenties, early thirties. It got to the point there was no one left for the gangs to steal from but each other. That goes on too long, all you got is a jungle, with the tigers left having to eat each other."

He picked up his bag and went through his whole routine twice. He threw his cigar butt in there after it. I was worried about fire, but when I heard the hiss, I knew it was wet enough in there to put the cigar out.

Gardeno leaned back in his chair. He put both hands on his chest, as if taking inventory of his heart and lungs.

"You know," he said, "I done some rotten stuff in my active

career. You want to know just what, you go back to New York and read that indictment. And maybe I ain't done doing rotten stuff. That remains to be seen."

And what, I wondered, did he mean by *that*?

Gardeno went on. "But there is one thing I never done. I never *ever* took nobody's legitimate business away. I never went into the napkin racket, or the jukebox racket, or protection, or any of that crap. Even when I'm a snot-nose kid running liquor, I knew that was suicide. Let legitimate business be. There was plenty of money to make in illegitimate business, if you know what I mean. There's a demand for something against the law, I fill it. Girls. Gambling. Juice. Whatever there was a market for."

"Drugs," I said.

Gardeno narrowed his eyes and stared hard at me for five seconds. Then he nodded slowly.

"Drugs, too," he said. "Back in the States, that is, before I come here and went legit. I keep saying that because you might be wired. I got the best lawyers on this island, and a couple from the States and from London, and they tell me as long as I stay clean, I can't be deported. St. David's don't care what I done before I came here to live."

The lenses went all brown again. "But yeah, in the old days, I smuggled drugs. I don't know if you'll believe me or not, and I'm not even sure I care, but I'm sorry I done it. See, I made two miscalculations. I thought only the colored would take the stuff, and I thought colored people were animals, so it didn't matter if they *did* take the stuff."

Kenni's voice was skeptical. "What made you change your mind?"

"Living here, where everybody's colored. Except this one young cop—boy, would he like to boot my tail out of here and into a Federal pen in the States—he's white."

I silently asked Buxton's forgiveness and let it pass.

"Like I was saying. Everyone's colored here, but none of the stuff I thought they did happens. I mean, they all live like people, you know what I mean? So there's gotta be other stuff going on in New York. Maybe here, if they're miserable, and they blame the government, they got only more colored guys to blame. I don't know what it is. But that's what made me change my mind. That and—"

Gardeno went into his coughing act, but his heart wasn't in it. He forgot to say "goddam" at the end, for one thing. It was as if he'd caught himself about to say too much, and was covering up.

It was easy enough to test When he had his breath back, I asked him, "And what?"

At least he wasn't coy about it "Never mind," he said. "Although I might tell you, at that. In a little while. You're an honest man. I can tell. Trouble with the world is too few honest men."

Since that came from an admitted lifelong criminal, I hardly knew what to say. I did know that while this afternoon was very educational, and would make a great magazine article if I were a magazine writer, I still had the irrational itch that had brought me here in the first place. Time to try a different tack.

"You said there were three reasons."

Gardeno coughed and spit, then said, "Hah?"

"Three reasons you let us in. The first was you wanted to talk about New York."

"Yeah. God, I get homesick I guess prison is worse than exile, but sometimes I wonder."

"What were the other two reasons?"

"Oh. No big deal. When Ray read me your card, like I said, he said you worked for the Network. I wanted to talk to you about TV, I watch it all the time, but the hell with that, now.

"The third thing was I recognized your name."

Kenni looked at me. She was only slightly less surprised than I was myself.

"You recognized *my* name?"

Gardeno shrugged. "I *think* so I suppose there could be more than one Matt Cobb who works for the Network You the guy who put Herschel Goldfarb away?"

"Oh," I said. "Was he a good friend of yours?"

Gardeno laughed, lost his breath, choked, turned purple, recovered "And now I'm gonna take revenge?" He laughed some more "Don't do this to me, you're going to kill me!" He sighed a few times "No," he said with the last sigh. "No, Goldfarb done some work for me—he's a financial genius, you know. And we've had a lawyer in common from time to time But no, he's no great friend of mine It's just that you hear talk. Even here, you hear talk. And the way Goldfarb has it, you did what two generations of cops couldn't do, and put him away. He says the only mistake he ever made was messing with you. So I sort of wanted to look you over. My eyes are bad, but I can see what he means."

"For God's sake!" Now I was getting this Superman crap from the *Mafia*. That could be extremely unhealthy. "Goldfarb kidnapped my girlfriend!" Gardeno looked at Kenni. "Not her," I said. "My ex-girlfriend. He made me come see him. He decided to have us blown away, then he went off with his mother and left two goons to do it. What was I supposed to do?"

Gardeno shrugged again. "A lot of guys would have died in that situation."

"I got lucky, that's all. For God's sake, he left his ledgers in the house! The D.A. didn't have a whole lot of trouble with him after that."

"Yeah, sure. Nothing special. You just took out two professional goons and recognized evidence when you saw it."

I was tired of arguing. "Forget it, okay? It was think of something or die, and I happened to think of something. That's all. Just let it go, all right?"

Gardeno raised a hand. There was still a memory of a smile on his thin lips. "All right, all right, we'll forget it. Instead, you tell me why you wanted to see *me* "

"I don't really know," I said honestly.

"Come on, come on. A young guy that has a beautiful girl don't go spending time with an old man, practically a corpse, for no reason. Look, Cobb, I don't have many afternoons left, but I spent one on you. You owe me "

It was my turn to shrug. "I guess it's because some incredibly nasty stuff has been going on on this trip. And you're here, and you've got a reputation I wondered if you have a few loose ends in your pockets."

"I don't have any loose ends, but I've had a lifetime of experience with nasty stuff Tell me the story."

"It's pretty complicated," I said

"I'm old," Gardeno said "Not stupid Talk "

He was old, he was feeble Practically a corpse, as he said himself But all of a sudden, I was afraid of him. I'd just had a look at the real Martin Gardeno, the one who'd built and run an empire He was not to be messed with.

I talked. "My involvement in the business starts with the disappearance—I found out today it was the murder—of a disk jockey who worked for the New York Network FM station. Joe Jenkins—real name Robert Joseph Janski—"

I didn't get any farther because Gardeno was having a fit.

"*Janski?* Janski's *dead*? He cheated me! That murdering son of a bitch bastard! He cheated me again! Goddam him!" He did not stop and ask Kenni to excuse him. He switched to Italian, and cursed the soul of Robert Joseph Janski until he passed out.

20

"A fit of what?"
"Pique. It means you were sore."
"Oh. Yeah, I was pique. I was pique as hell."
—Burl Ives and Hal Buckley, "O.K. Crackerby!" (ABC)

Martin Gardeno tossed his head against the bleached linen on the hospital bed as if looking for a place to spit. This was another part of the estate he'd spent a fortune on—a fully equipped hospital room, complete with a semiprivate doctor, who had his own house (and practice) elsewhere on the estate. Gardeno let him stay there, rent-free, on the understanding that he never be more than five minutes away from his American patient.

I felt relieved to hear about these arrangements. It meant that Gardeno's choking himself into unconsciousness was a more or less regular occurrence, and we were unlikely to be blamed for nearly snuffing the old man.

I was especially glad, because I wanted to talk to him some more. Of all the connections I might have guessed at in the mess my life had become since the *Caribbean Comet* had steamed out of New York Harbor, the last one would have been Joe Jenkins–Martin Gardeno. I had to hear more about this.

Fortunately, by the time the doctor got around to thinking of throwing us out, Gardeno had come around and was insisting on seeing us. Actually, as the doctor made clear, he had specified only me, but Kenni made it equally clear that she was not going to be moved from my side. That was flattering. I only hoped Gardeno wouldn't find it inhibiting.

He didn't. He looked at her, smiled, and said he knew she'd be with me. He said if he had found a woman like her, he might not have been a bachelor all his life.

Then he asked us to stand clear of the TV sets, an array of which

147

was set up at the foot of the bed, sharing space on a rack with sophisticated diagnostic equipment.

A lot of the equipment was hooked up to him, but he paid no attention to the monitors. He was more interested in a ridiculously young Burt Reynolds in some dumb war movie on Channel 9 out of Secaucus, New Jersey. He wasn't very interested in that, either.

"I hate this room," he said. "This damn tube in my nose. Oxygen. Know what that means?"

"You won't turn purple so much," Kenni offered.

"It means no cigars, either. I'll be in here two or three days, no cigars. I should have another room in this place padded like a nuthouse for me to stay in after I go three days with no cigars."

"They're trying to keep you alive," Kenni said.

Gardeno looked down the sheet at his gnarled hands. "I know they are. But they ain't the ones who done it. *I* been keeping me alive. Willpower. The same way I done everything else in my life. Willpower. Because I had to wait until Janski came back to this island. I knew he would. And then I'd get him, and I'd make him talk, and I'd find out who his partner was, and then I could die in peace. I mean, I don't know what my soul faces from God, but I made my own choices, you know? Besides, maybe there isn't any God, and I come out ahead of all the poor suckers who lived on peanuts because they were afraid of what would happen after.

"But what I been afraid of is leaving this job undone. That's why I wanted to talk to you, Cobb. I want you to do me a favor."

"I don't think I do your kind of favors, Mr. Gardeno."

"Hear me out, then decide."

The doctor popped his face in and gave us a dirty look. Gardeno told him to get the hell out of there, and began to talk.

Martin Gardeno never married, but he never lacked for women in his life. For fun, there were the girls in his houses, or there were just girls who liked to hang around with a guy who had money and didn't care to ask any questions about where the money came from. With them, he kept it casual, bought them nice presents, treated them nice (by which he meant he didn't beat them), and moved on when he wanted a change, no hard feelings.

But a man needed a home made for him, too. That was another big reason he never got married. There were only two women in the world he knew of who were interested in keeping a home for a man the way the home ought to be kept—his mother and his sister, God rest their souls.

When his mother died, he and his sister Angela just kept living in the same house in Greenpoint. Gardeno supported the family, and everything was fine.

Everything was still fine when Angela married a guy named Sam Veria. A good guy. A straight guy. Owned a couple of taxicabs, made a decent living himself, in every sense of the word. Loved Angela, she loved him. Good husband. Good brother-in-law. Good father to little Marty, a smart little kid who looked just like his mother. Gardeno was his godfather.

One day—middle of the afternoon—Sam was out driving one of the cabs. He didn't have to do that, but he liked to—said it made for a better relationship with his drivers—when he got killed by some doped-up punk who dropped a chunk of concrete off an overpass on the Cross-Bronx Expressway through Sam's windshield. Gardeno put all his influence to work, but the punk was never found.

Angela made up for the loss of her husband by doubling the amount of love she poured onto her son. At least once a day, she made her brother promise that he would look out for the kid, help him through life.

It used to make Gardeno mad. He was the kid's godfather wasn't he? And his uncle, too? Of *course* he'd take Marty under his wing.

In fact, he might have taken the kid under his wing if he'd only been the child of a casual acquaintance. Marty Veria was *sharp*. He started working for his uncle at the age of seventeen. He streamlined the numbers operation so as to increase profits by almost two percent. That's no insignificant figure when you're talking about millions of dollars a day.

And Marty figured out the drug delivery system. Marty had contempt for anybody who used drugs, and he didn't forget his father. He just realized that the punk who dropped the rock would have gotten the dope *somewhere*, no matter who was selling it.

So Marty Veria (with financial backing from his uncle) set up a dope operation. The idea was to use free-lancers, who would take all the risks, financial and physical, as far as the Caribbean. It was so easy to smuggle stuff in from the Caribbean, Marty knew, that his uncle's resources could take it from there.

Unfortunately, free-lancers were usually nervous, to say nothing of paranoid, and while the preliminary deals were set up through intermediaries, leaving Marty out of it, it was still desirable to have as few of these people arrested as possible. The more people the various police agencies got to question, the more they might be able to put together.

So Marty put together an elaborate payoff system. He and the free-lancer would meet on Claxton's Island, a short seaplane hop from Davidstown. Marty would check the stuff for quality, then the free-lancer would stash it, or leave it with someone he trusted. Then they'd go, completely clean, to St. David's Island, where Marty would remove diamonds from a numbered safe-deposit box in one of the island's anonymous banks. Then they'd go back, retrieve the stuff, make the exchange, and go their separate ways. It wasn't perfect, but it was better than most systems. And, as Marty told each free-lancer, he was making too much money to double-cross anybody.

"Then he worked a deal with this Janski," Gardeno said. "And I never saw my nephew again. The guy waited at the bank and waited, and Marty never showed up. They finally found him under a pile of rocks on Claxton's Island."

"A burn," I said.

"To hell with the burn. They wanted to keep the drugs, all they had to do was keep the drugs. No skin off my ass, or Marty's either. They were after something else."

The dawn broke. "How much was in that numbered box?"

"Still is. Marty was the only one who knew the number. He kept changing it after every operation."

"So it's still there," Kenni breathed.

"Five million dollars in diamonds. At the price then. Less a couple hundred grand paid for a few operations. God knows what they're worth now."

"That's why you knew Janski would come back."

"That's why I knew."

"But why are you so sure they got the number out of your nephew before they killed him?"

" 'Cause he was tortured. You want to hear what they done to him? It involved a lot of cigarettes and my nephew's naked body. Seems he talked right after they burned out one of his eyes—sorry, Miss, but you insisted on coming in here."

Kenni swallowed hard and nodded.

"Okay, then," Gardeno went on. "They tortured him, but he didn't die of the torture. He died from having—"

"Having the back of his skull crushed with a rock," I said. "A blow to the occipital bone from below."

"How did you know that?" Gardeno demanded. He might have been half dead, but right now he was also deadly.

"There's been a lot of it going around," I said. "If it makes you feel any better, that's exactly the way Janski died."

"It doesn't make me feel a damn bit better. It just means the partner's the one who killed my nephew, and he finally turned on Janski, too."

Kenni, the irrepressible mystery fan, had been puzzling over something. Now she brightened and said, "Ah. If he hadn't told them the number, they just would have kept on torturing him until he died. Since they ended it abruptly, they must have gotten what they wanted."

"Yeah," Gardeno said. "Because I was under indictment in New York, and the D.A. had a good case, and I couldn't get bail. They figured they could walk into the bank and get the money and take off and start a new life somewhere, and I wouldn't be able to do a damn thing about it."

Gardeno pulled oxygen into his lungs, inhaling so hard, I thought he was going to suck up the whole rubber tube.

"Let me tell you something. If I'd stood trial, I would have walked. The fix was in. I'm not gonna tell you how, or with who, but it was set for Gardeno to be acquitted. I was ready to retire, anyway. I would have gone back to Brooklyn and consoled my sister. I would have lived in civilization.

"But I couldn't afford to wait. I didn't *want* to wait. When that Janski showed up, I was going to be the one asking the questions, giving the pain if I didn't get the name of that partner. I was going to be the one to blow him away. That was worth walking out on a sure thing for. That was worth this goddam exile, with nothing but TV to take me back to the city."

Gardeno clawed at the bedding. "Without me, without her son, my sister died in two years. I couldn't even go to her funeral. I owed Janski. I owe his partner. Now I'll probably never be able to pay."

About this point, I had to remind myself that Gardeno was no prize as a human being. Not to put too fine a point on it, he was undoubtedly a murderous scumbag. But loyalty to family and determination in the face of adversity are two qualities I regard highly. Gardeno hadn't made me his friend, but he had fascinated me in spite of myself. A glance at Kenni showed me she was feeling the same way.

"You must have done other things to find him," I said. "You didn't just sit here and wait."

"No, I didn't just sit here and wait. I pulled every string I knew how. I had the whole outfit searching the world for him. I even did stupid things."

Kenni shot me a look. Gardeno didn't notice.

"I sent this colored kid to college, numbers runner for us, smart boy. I sent him to NYU to spy in case Janski was stupid enough to try to go back."

"NYU?" I said. I remembered the old Red Skelton answer to that—NY *not* me?—but I put it from my mind. "Janski was at NYU?"

"Yeah. He was old for a student, but he'd been booted out of somewhere a few years before because he sold some coke. He got a suspended sentence or something, came to New York, and NYU let him in."

My mind was spinning. It had taken a long time for the connections to come, but Gardeno had some doozies. Gardeno and Janski. Janski and NYU.

"You don't happen to know if Janski had something to do with a Professor Schaeffer, do you? Lee H. Schaeffer?"

"The mystery writer? The guy who invented that private eye show? He taught at NYU?"

"He certainly did," I said. I pressed on, but while Gardeno had had thorough research done on Robert Joseph Janski, it wasn't anything I didn't know from vetting him for the Network. I found it interesting that the one thing Janski had managed to keep hidden from us was his stint at NYU. That, and the fact that he'd apparently once been a torture murderer.

Gardeno was morose. "I can't believe it," he said. "God, he was a bastard, wasn't he?"

I was busy thinking. Gardeno took it for reproach.

"Okay. I'm no better. But I don't think you think Janski and his friend should get away with what they done."

"Janski didn't get away with it. He only got away from you."

"The partner, then. Cobb, like I said before, there's something I want you to do for me."

"I'm not going to do anything for you."

I looked at Gardeno's face and was amazed. The old man was hurt by my rejection. I wondered what the hell he expected.

"Okay," he said. "Don't do it for me. Do it for justice. Do it for ten percent of the value of the diamonds in that box."

I opened my mouth, but Gardeno cut me off. "Not for you, personally. For charity. You name it. Or don't name it. What time does your ship sail?"

"Tomorrow afternoon," I said. Buxton willing.

"Okay. Tomorrow morning, my lawyer will be at the ship, setting it all up. You can fill in the name of the charity. Or change your mind and keep the money."

"No," I said.

"Why don't you find out what I want you to do?"

"You might as well listen to that much, Matt," Kenni said.

I looked at her. We'd been close for a few days, but did I really know her? A lot of people's brains stop working in the vicinity of large sums of money. Working at the Network is no good for anybody's mental health, but one thing it does do is get you thinking of five hundred thousand dollars as not much. You can't produce a sitcom for two weeks for the Network on five hundred thousand dollars.

"What do you want me to do?" I said.

"Don't let it drop. Even if I die, don't let it drop. Keep on this. Keep after Janski's partner."

"Janski's partner may have nothing to do with my problems."

Gardeno lifted his head from the pillow and fixed me with his eyes. "I'm a dying man," he said. "Don't waste my time. The shots to the head? My nephew? Janski?"

He was right of course. His nephew, Janski, and Watson Burkehart, too. Copycat killers have been known to exist, but in order to copy the technique of a previous murder, you have to know it happened. Janski's body hadn't been discovered until after Burkehart was killed and, Gardeno was telling me now, the details of his nephew's death had never been released.

"So I keep after Janski's partner, and then what?"

"Then you do the right thing. That's all I ask."

"I do the right thing," I said.

"Didn't I just say I want you for this because I can tell you're an honest man? What do you think, I want to make a goddam *torpedo* out of you? You do the right thing. If you got a case for the cops, go to the cops. If I'm alive and you need me, I'll come and testify and die in jail. At least I'll be home. If you don't have a case for the cops, think of something. I tell you, I know about you. Don't do nothing to hurt your conscience. Just hurt this bastard friend of Janski's."

"Okay," I said.

"You agree?" Gardeno seemed surprised.

"Why not? It's exactly what I was going to do, anyway. Tell your lawyer the money goes to the New York Public Library."

Kenni gasped. Gardeno laughed at her, coughed, then laughed some more. He was still smiling as he drifted off to sleep.

21

Buxton let us sail. Not, mind you, before he had taken everybody's name and address (from passports—he was taking nobody's word for anything) and extracted approximately a thousand solemn vows to cooperate if their local police contacted them on his behalf with further inquiries in the matter. There was some grumbling about it being a lousy way to spend your last morning on the island, especially since we'd only been there a couple of days, but everybody went along. A lot of them probably thought it was still part of the mystery game.

Buxton had a few words with me, too. I filled him in on the state of Martin Gardeno. He got excited.

"This means the whole time he's been on St. David's Island, he's been conspiring to commit a crime." He was instantly depressed. "But I couldn't make anything of that, could I?"

"He could say he was teasing us."

"Precisely. And it would take the lawyers years to prove any overt action had been taken in furtherance of the conspiracy."

He got technical for a while, and I tuned him out. Gardeno's lawyer had delivered that morning a three-inch-thick stack of legal technicalities. Thank God I didn't have to sign it, because then I would have had to read it. I'd been impressed, though, with the sheer *volume* of the thing. Either Gardeno had told his lawyers to keep something like this ready in case an honest man showed up, or the old man demanded and got a level of service only the most extravagant expenditure of money can secure.

Anyway, the idea was to hand that over to a lawyer in New York,

155

and the New York Public Library could keep a few branches open a few more weeks.

In the middle of everything, I received a message telling me Mr. Maxwell of the American Embassy wanted to see me. I let him speak to Mr. Buxton, of the Royal St. David's Island Constabulary, who told him I could not be spared before sailing time. Maxwell then apparently got huffy about my rights as an American, which was big of him, but Buxton told him I had volunteered to stay put and that I had made no request to see anyone from the Embassy.

Then damned if Maxwell doesn't come to the ship to see me. He was not pleased with me. I had told him I didn't know Mr. Gardeno, but there I was yesterday, calling on him. Me and Miss Clayton.

Usually, when it becomes my fate to be involved in something like this, I wind up lying to the authorities about something in one way or another. Not this time. I just opened the bag for Maxwell. I didn't even ask why a cultural attaché would want to know this stuff. I told him everything I'd told Buxton, and I learned something. It's not that honesty isn't the best policy, it's that sometimes it makes no damn difference at all. Maxwell was every bit as suspicious, hostile, and obnoxious as he would have been if I'd been setting out a line of whoppers for him. I think it really bothered him that with his cover, he couldn't actually threaten me. At last, he went away, suppressing grumbles.

I was in my cabin with Kenni when the ship sailed, doing something a lot more entertaining than waving to the folks on the pier. The throbbing of a steam engine is better than a vibrating bed. At an appropriate moment, the ship's whistle blew. Kenni said, "Wow," and we both laughed.

Then she put her face close to mine. "How do you feel about clichés?" she said.

"Clichés? I hate them like poison."

"I'm serious, Matt."

I didn't know what she was talking about, so I just said, "Okay. Me too. Go ahead."

She nodded. "Here it is, the big cliché question: Will you call me when we get back to New York?"

"You'll just have to wait and see, won't you?"

Kenni said, "Oh."

"Hold it," I said. "Hold it. That didn't go over right. All I meant was, the rest of the cliché is that the guy says yes, then doesn't do it, so what good would it do me to answer?"

"It could give me the rest of the trip to work up reasons to hate you. Or keep me happy for the rest of the trip."

"Well, actually, what I was planning to do when we got to New York was to make calling you superfluous by taking you directly to my apartment."

"You mean that?"

"I've got a lot of bad habits," I told her, "but toying with people—good people, anyway—has never been one of them. Of course I mean it."

"You asked for it," she said. "You're going to have a tough time getting rid of me now, buster." Then she kissed me, hard, and Kenni, I, and the S.S. *Caribbean Comet* steamed off into the ocean.

The Atlantic started to get nasty at dinnertime. Tropical Storm Jason, this time. It wasn't too bad at first, but by the end of the meal you had to time your eating to those instants the waves threw you and your plate into sync.

It didn't affect conversation, though.

"The big solution comes tomorrow," Neil Furst said.

"I wish," I said, and everybody laughed.

"I mean of the mystery game. I think Grandma did it."

"Shame on you," Althea Nell Furst said. "What a disloyal child." But she was beaming on him all the same.

Jan said, "I wonder if we'll ever find out about that other stuff."

"Leave the guy alone," Mike Ryerson said. "Can't you see he's worn out from working on the case?" Rough seas and all, Mike looked a lot happier than he had the other day, and Judy was positively blissful. Not so blissful, however, that she neglected to give him a subtle kick under the table. It made him grin. When he saw how his remark had made Kenni blush, he grinned some more.

More to change the subject than anything else, I answered Jan's question.

"I don't know if we're ever going to know for sure what the hell's been going on here, but I know where to look."

"Where?"

"In the past. Janski's, Schaeffer's, everybody else we can think of." What with Kenni, me, and general gossip, the inner circle was up to date on our visit to Gardeno. "For instance, the Network executive who wished this trip on me. Is he tied in with these people somewhere?"

"How can you do that?" Jan wanted to know.

Mrs. Furst smiled at her. "Goodness, dear, you really are *not* a mystery fan, are you? There are dozens of ways. Tax records, old phone books, voter lists—"

"Registrar's offices, old newspapers," I went on. "It's going to be one of those dusty, boring jobs I hate. Fortunately, I have good people I can put on it."

"Is your boss going to let you do that?" Neil Furst asked.

"He's going to insist on it. Schaeffer was published by a subsidiary of the Network."

"I didn't know that," Jan said.

"Neither did I. Or I had forgotten. I would have been nicer to him."

"You keep talking about him in the past tense," Mrs. Furst said. "You're convinced he's dead then."

I looked at the kid. He was taking it all in; but if his grandmother didn't mind this kind of talk in front of him, neither did I.

"I'm afraid so," I said. "And if he's not, when I catch up with him, he's going to wish he was."

And on that rather ambiguous note, dinner broke up. Just as well, because that was when Jason decided really to cut loose. The ship started to jump so much I was sure it was going to curve in the middle, like a banana. The companionways were carpeted hills one second, carpeted ski slopes the next. Stairways went horizontal and wiggled from side to side. My main goal in life was to make it back to my cabin, to my own private head, before losing my dinner. The smells and other evidences of the many who had not didn't make things any easier.

Kissing Kenni at the door of her cabin did, though, help take my mind off it, and I made it the last few yards down the hallway, once again calling myself a fool for going anywhere near an ocean during hurricane season. I consoled myself with the notion that if the ship sank I wouldn't have to worry about Janski, Schaeffer, and the mysterious partner. I fumbled the key into a lock that kept jumping away from my hands, and staggered inside.

Call it a moral victory. I made it to the head, but the ship lurched, and I wound up messing myself. To hell with it, I thought. I pulled my clothes off, got the Dramamine from the medicine cabinet, crunched a couple like M&Ms, avoided throwing up again only because there was nothing to throw, and lurched to the bed. Spot came and lay sympathetically beside me. I was glad to have him, if only because he kept me from rolling out of the bunk.

I don't know if it was the drug or lying flat that did it, but in a little while, I felt a lot better. Not great, mind you. I had simply reached a point where I now actually hoped I would live through this. Until now, I had been vacillating between complete indifference and a passionate desire to die.

It got awfully hot in the room, after a while. Close. I guess the ship had enough to worry about in keeping the engines churning the froth out there without making the air-conditioning a major concern.

But I was in hypochondriac heaven, with nothing to worry about *but* the state of my comfort. I decided I needed some air. I pulled some clothes from my laundry basket. I wound up with a shirt from yesterday and the pants I'd been wearing the day after Schaeffer disappeared, when Kenni and I had searched his cabin. I didn't bother with socks. I let Spot have the whole bunk, which he was delighted to take, and made my way up to B deck, holding onto the wall as if it were my best friend.

I was surprised at the number of people I passed; people, I supposed, who were immune to motion sickness, or compelled by machismo or other lunacy to pretend they were. Some of them wanted to talk to me, undoubtedly wanting to know what the Clue of the Angry Chef meant, or how Billy and Karen had gotten the St. David's Island Police to pretend that someone had been actually murdered. I waved everybody off and opened a glass door to the outside.

It wasn't worth it. I found out the air conditioner *had* been working in my cabin, and doing a hell of a job, too. It took this fetid, hot, wet muck that reminded me of trying to breathe clam juice, and turned it into something that was merely stuffy. I turned to go back inside.

Thirty seconds later, I was nose down to the ocean and about to go over.

22

"Let's do it to them before they do it to us."
—Robert Proski, "Hill Street Blues" (NBC)

I crammed more thinking into the next few seconds than I had done in four years of college. The killer had leverage; I had strength. Did I have enough strength to hang by my hands from a rail? Sure, I did. Did I have enough strength to hang by my hands from a *wet* rail? After being hit on the head? With someone trying to make me let go? That was going to take experimentation, and I only had one chance.

On the other hand, that one chance was a chance to live. Failing that, it was a chance at revenge. Revenge can be very attractive at a time like that.

So, I thought, you keep pushing me toward the ocean, let's do what *you* want to do for a change. I fought hard to get my feet down to the deck. I wanted as much purchase as I could get, and I wanted my playmate pushing at maximum. Then, as the ship rolled in that direction, I kicked up and over the rail. The idea was to hook legs under my friend's armpits, drag the killer over with me, let go, and feed the bastard to the fish. Then (God willing), I'd clamber back onto the ship.

It didn't quite work. My friend caught wise to what I was doing and broke free just as my body went sideways over the rail. I held tight The ship kept rolling that way, the base of the wall tilting in and away from me, leaving me blowing in the wind like a flag. The wind tried to tear me from my hold, but I forced all my energy into my fingers, telling myself this would be the worst of it, if I could just hold on until the ship came back . . .

And it did, not a second too soon. I put my feet out to meet it, and held on until the slant was almost maximum. I clambered up It

160

wasn't too bad, just plenty bad enough, like trying to get out of a muddy ditch in a rainstorm. I pulled myself over the railing, and collapsed on the deck, sliding back and forth like a shuffleboard disk while I tried to catch my breath.

I strained to hear footsteps or other ominous sounds through the wind, but couldn't catch anything. Apparently, I'd been given up for dead. Or maybe my friend didn't like it out here any more than I did. I crawled along the deck until I found another door. I pulled myself to my feet, fought the door open against the wind, and went inside.

People who weren't too nauseated to be curious stared at me. I didn't blame them. Next to me, a drowned rat would look like Lassie. I smiled at them. I'd gone quite a way when I realized I wasn't seasick anymore.

I was laughing as I went into sick bay.

The next day, I was ill. Very ill. I'd be confined to sick bay, or my cabin, for the rest of the voyage. Apparently, I had gone out on the bridge for some air, foolish man, and had slipped and bashed my head against the deck. That, the doctor told everyone who asked, is all Mr. Cobb remembers of the incident. This sort of traumatic amnesia is not unusual in cases like this; with rest, Mr. Cobb should be fine.

I had visitors. Jan and Kenni brought Spot. Kenni said it was suspicious that I should have smashed my head in just that place, and I should try to remember. I promised I would. Jan and Spot both made sympathetic noises, but only Spot licked my face.

Billy and Karen and all the mystery writers came by and hoped I was okay. Billy couldn't stop apologizing, as if it was his fault.

"Forget it," I said. "You're not the one who hit me in the head. As strong as you are, with a black belt and all, I wouldn't just have a minor case of amnesia."

Right, I thought. If my thoughts had only gone in that direction as soon as I'd seen Burkehart's body, I could have saved a lot of grief.

I wound up with a lot of autographed mysteries to read, and lots of cards and chachkas from the ship's gift shop.

I also heard a lot of Frank Sinatra music. Dr. Sato did have a good voice. I put up with it until two o'clock that afternoon. That was the time of the mandatory landing briefing, where the social director gathered everyone (except obvious invalids like me) and told them to throw the rest of the marijuana they scored on the island overboard, and how it was incumbent on New York State residents to go to Albany and pay the state sales tax on anything they bought while out of state. Try to enforce that one.

About the time it was to start, I asked to see the purser.

Dr. Sato looked at me. "You want to see the purser."

"Right."

He took out his little penlight and checked my eyes.

"I'm not delirious," I said.

"No, and you haven't lost your memory, either, have you?"

"No," I admitted, "I haven't. How can you tell?" If I'd done that bad a job of faking it, I was in trouble.

"It doesn't worry you enough," the doctor said. "Landlubbers lose their footing a lot on shipboard, and some of them lose their memory temporarily when they hit their heads. But, Mr. Cobb, in all my experience, no one ever loses his memory without being desperate to get it back. You show no signs of desperation. Therefore, I feel you remember exactly what happened to you last night."

I sure did. I remembered having nothing below me but ocean, and I shuddered.

"Why are you feigning amnesia to all your friends, Mr. Cobb?"

"Because I'm trying to make someone feel secure. Do I get to talk to the purser?"

Sato looked at me. "I will ring him. I will be discreet. And I am sure the purser will join me in saying that we will be glad to see the last of you and your mystery-monger friends."

That wasn't fair, and I would have told him so, if I hadn't needed more favors from him. As it was, I spent the interval making plans, and listening to the doctor croon "One for My Baby, and One More for the Road."

Once again, the purser gave me the key to Schaeffer's cabin and turned me loose. The burn mark on the carpet was still there. So were all of Schaeffer's things. Or rather one very important item was missing, but it had been missing the first time I'd searched the place, too. I'd just been too stupid to register its absence. Nobody got that kind of bald spot coverage without a *blow dryer*. We'd spent a lot of time talking about Schaeffer's blow-dried coif. But there was no such implement in this cabin. I knew now where it was—at the bottom of the Atlantic, along with the knife set Burkehart stole. I knew where they were, and I knew what they had been used for; and though sometime in the night the ship had passed through the storm, and the sea was now calm and gentle, I still felt a little queasy.

This wasn't getting the job done. I went to Schaeffer's bathroom and got busy. Dr. Sato furnished me with absorbent cotton and some specimen bottles. I knelt and got to work. I tore off a goodly hunk of cotton and wiped it around inside the drain of the stainless steel tub. I put it in the bottle and labeled it. I did the same for the toilet and sink, though they would be less likely to produce results.

I sighed. If I produced any results, it wouldn't mean much. It wouldn't come anywhere near a corpus delicti. Still, it would be an indication that I was on the right track. I had begun to suspect that last night, when I thought I had been about to die. I was so angry at the thought of dying without knowing what was going on, my imagination had just cooked up a nice story for me, so I'd go happy into the drink. Now I was stuck with it, and I wanted to make as certain as possible I was right before I took any action. Assuming, of course, that I could think of any action to take.

I labeled up the jar from the sink, and got to my feet. Then it occurred to me that blood that got rinsed from the mouth of the drain might well wind up deeper in the pipes, in the trap, say. I didn't have a wrench or a plumber's snake, so I'd have to improvise.

I opened Schaeffer's closet and took out a wire coat hanger. I was glad I did, because I noticed something else—or rather the lack of something else—that I'd missed the day before. The clothes still smelled of recent dry cleaning. Not as strongly as they had before, but strong enough. That much was fine. I'd had a lot of my stuff cleaned before the trip, too. But *I* was ass deep in plastic film. Where was the plastic film off Schaeffer's clothes? He might have skinned it all off and thrown it away, but he hadn't done it before he'd come on board, or the smell would have dissipated by now.

I took a chance of being discovered and went to find Chiun. Yes, Mr. Schaeffer had many dry-cleaned clothes when he came aboard. No, Chiun had not removed any plastic films from the garbage in Mr. Schaeffer's cabin, the one night there'd been any. Chiun was sure of this, because the plastic film gummed up the ship's incinerator if you tried to burn it, so they usually dumped it overboard, though they weren't supposed to.

"Now you know steward's guilty secret," Chiun said. "Do I give you money to keep quiet?" He grinned at the idea of giving money to a passenger. When I reached into my pocket and worked the transaction the usual way, the grin widened. I told Chiun the money was so that he would forget I was ever here. He nodded and said, "Why am I standing here talking to myself?" and walked away.

I went back to the cabin and did a deeper swab of the bathtub drains. I labeled those, and brought the whole mess down to Dr. Sato.

The doctor ran blood tests to the strains of "Cycles," singing along.

"Human blood," he said, as the fluid in a test tube turned a pale blue. "That's all I can tell you from a sample this size."

"Where?"

"From the one you labeled 'Tub drain—top,' a little. From 'Tub drain—deep,' considerably more."

I rubbed my chin. "Some men shave in the shower, but—"

"A man who shaves in the shower cannot avoid leaving hairs in the drain, Mr. Cobb." Put a few pounds on him, change his accent, and he could have been Charlie Chan. "There were no such hairs in the sample you brought me, just loose head hairs, such as a balding man might leave. Also, the percentage of blood cells was far too high to have been left by anything but the most severe cut. Much worse than a man is likely to give himself while shaving."

"Good," I said magnanimously. "I had been about to say that Schaeffer used an electric razor, anyway, but you sound a lot more convincing. Hold on to those specimens, will you, Doctor?"

"I will, of course. But I have only given you my opinions. I doubt that I could qualify as an expert in any court."

"I can find experts if I need them. You've helped me a lot."

"I am always delighted to be of help to the passengers," he said. "I now pronounce you well enough to return to your cabin. Relax. Take your meals there. You are not to engage in acrobatics. Not on deck with an attacker, nor in bed. Do you understand me?"

"Absolutely," I said. "I want to make this look good, too."

Dr. Sato was getting exasperated. "I don't have the slightest interest in making anything 'look good.' I have given you serious medical advice. You are recovering from a concussion. Granted it was a mild one, head injuries can be tricky. A blow that gives one man some minor inconvenience might kill another. I strongly urge you to see your own physician as soon as possible after we make port."

I said I would, thanked him, and found my way out. I left him and Frankie proclaiming they would roll themselves up in a big ball and die, my, my.

I took the doctor's advice and stayed in my cabin until I absolutely had to leave. Kenni came and took Spot for walks, and fluffed my pillow, etc. I kept reminding myself that Kenni was in no danger. The killer was a psychopath, not a fool. There was nothing to be feared from Kenni, and the best way to keep things that way was to keep our contact to a minimum. I had come up with a plan; all I had to do now was convince myself to go through with it.

Finally, Kenni came and summoned me to the big ballroom upstairs. Customs and Immigration were processing people on the ship, instead of making them wait in line in a drafty shed while everything got checked out. I rejoined the gang one last time. We sat and drank coffee until they called our cabin numbers.

Everybody but me wanted to talk about the real-life mystery—the disappearance of the writer, the death of the nasty dining room steward. I was grateful for the almost constant interruptions by mystery cruisers coming to thank Karen and Billy for "more fun than I've had in years," or "the time of our lives," to give a few random quotes.

"God is good," Billy said.

Karen was so happy she was practically laughing. "We came up with a solution—sort of. It was so ridiculous and farfetched, I was afraid they were going to send us to Davy Smith's locker."

"Davy *Jones's* locker," Phil DeGrave said.

Karen asked him if he was sure, but didn't wait for an answer. She went on, "Instead, they *loved* it!" She started explaining the solution, but since I'd lost track of the mystery after the first day, I tuned out right after she told me that Bob Madison had set a murder trap for himself in order to frame the prize hen who had laid the eggs. After that, it *really* got farfetched.

Billy kept shaking his head. "The real solution was so *good*. It made *sense*. Ellery Queen would have been proud of it."

"Use it the next time," Mike Ryerson said. He was back to being his bluff, hearty self. "Nobody knows what it is, so it's still good."

"Or write it up as a book," Nicola Andrews said.

Billy would not be consoled. "Maybe we should look into science-fiction cruises."

Karen gasped. "What a great idea!" And she was off and planning. They started calling our group off through Customs. I spent the time examining my conclusions for holes. I didn't find any. I wasn't sure that meant there *weren't* any, or just that my bottle-softened brain was too weak to find them.

Just before it was my turn to go through Customs, Phil DeGrave said, "Too bad we couldn't shed some light on the other thing."

"Yeah," I said. "Well, sometimes you slay the beast, and sometimes the beast slays you."

"It's a lot easier the way we do it," Althea Nell Furst said. "When you make up the crime *and* the criminal, solving it is child's play."

They called my number. I shook hands all around and went. The customs people made a fuss over Spot. At first I thought they suspected me of smuggling dogs, or possibly dog collars, into the States, but they were only bowled over by his canine beauty.

Kenni and Jan had been called a few minutes ago. Kenni was already through. Jan was taking much longer because she had forms to fill out. She had some parcels full of island weaving she wanted to display in her store to see if there was a market for it on the trendy Upper West Side, and she had to pay extra taxes or whatever.

Finally, they were done with her, and she came over to us.

"There's a Network limo waiting," I said. "To take you home."

"Oh," she said. "Aren't you coming with us, Matt?"

Kenni blushed again and made a little harumph. "Ahh, actually, Jan, I'm going to Matt's place. He's still a little woozy, and someone has to walk Spot—"

Jan smiled a bless-you-my-children smile. "It's just as well. And listen, you two take the limo."

"It's for you," I insisted. "You're the contest winner."

"I've got a few errands to run before I go home, anyway. I'll be better off in a cab."

"The driver will take you on your errands. The Network can afford it."

"No, I'd just as soon do it this way. I insist. My prerogative as a contest winner."

I conceded, grudgingly. Jan stood on tiptoe to kiss Kenni on the cheek. They promised to see each other later.

Jan turned to me. "Thanks for everything, Matt. It's been so nice to meet you. I know this trip has been a mess for you. Did you ever talk to those people from the island tourist bureau?"

"They canceled me."

"Oh," she said. "I hope your deal goes through."

"It will. Too much money, too many perks at stake for both sides."

"Anyway, I want you to know that in spite of everything, I've really had a wonderful time."

She smiled warmly and put out her hand. I took it and said, "You know, Jan," I said, "I believe you really mean that."

"I really do, Matt."

I looked at her. "Good," I said sincerely. "That takes a load off my mind."

23

"Trust me—I know what I'm doing."
—David Rasche, "Sledge Hammer" (ABC)

It would have warmed the mayor's heart to see how happy Spot was to be back in New York. He kept scooting from one side of the limo to the other, taking it all in. I was glad he was pleased. He'd have to earn his Alpo before the day was out.

When we got to the apartment on Central Park West, Kenni went to take a shower, and I started making phone calls. I was surprised to see that St. David's Island did not have its own area code, but shared one with the rest of that part of the Caribbean.

The whole business took about an hour. Not because it was so hard to get through (it wasn't), but because I had a lot to say, and I had to say it three times. I made one more call, a local one. I had a job for Harris Brophy, and I wanted to get him to work on it right away.

Kenni came into the living room toweling her hair. She was wearing a gold silk robe that belonged to Jane Sloan. Jane is not a large woman, and on Kenni, the robe looked more like a gift wrap than a garment.

"You look," I said, "indecently delicious."

"That was more or less the idea," she told me. "This is quite a place. I've been looking at the bedrooms."

"Yeah," I said. "Hold that thought. Spot and I have to go out."

Kenni's face fell. "Oh. Are you going to be gone long?"

"No," I said. "Not long."

"Good. I'll take a nap and warm the bed up."

I told her that sounded like a good idea. I didn't say I hoped she still liked touching me when I came back and told her what I'd been up to. I kissed her and left.

168

* * *

Wooly Thinking was on Columbus Avenue, north of Seventy-ninth Street, set between an expensive hairstylist and a gourmet coffee shop. The door was locked when I got there, but I looked through the glass and saw luggage where its owner had dumped it. I stood outside and smelled coffee while Spot and I waited. It occurred to me that Kenni's coffee had been doctored the night before we reached the island. I had forgotten all about that. But it fit. It fit fine. Kenni had been poisoned to keep her and me on the ship next day. More specifically, to keep us from going ashore. Because Kenni and Jan and I were more or less a threesome. We might have expected to do that first day on the island together. And Jan couldn't have that. So she'd risked Kenni's life to make sure it didn't happen. It made Jan out to be a callous bitch, but that was the least of it.

It wasn't long before she came back. Irritation flashed across her face almost too quickly to notice, replaced immediately by a glowing smile.

"Matt," she said. "What a nice surprise."

"I've got something important to tell you. Mind if I come in?"

"Not at all." She unlocked the door and waved me inside. The still-sore lump at the back of my head tingled a little at the thought of letting her behind me, but logic won. It was a busy neighborhood and a busy street. Too many people walking by for her to risk it. Besides, I had Spot to protect me.

"Come into my office," she said. She led the way this time. I followed closely enough to make sure she didn't have a chance to prepare a reception for me. She pulled some fabric samples off a chair, and asked me to sit. Spot squatted at my feet. She took the swivel chair behind her desk. I looked around, making sure there was no back way out of the shop. There wasn't.

"It's nice that banks are open Saturdays these days, isn't it?" I said.

"Very convenient," she agreed. "But how did you know I've been to the bank?"

"You mentioned it down at the docks. I wonder," I said, "what I would find if I searched you right now?"

She grinned slyly. She was a damned attractive woman. "It's an appealing idea, Matt, but what would Kenni say?"

I ignored her. "I know I wouldn't find the diamonds. They're in a safe-deposit box at the bank, at some bank that's open Saturdays. It would be hard to find. Would I find a deposit box receipt on you, maybe in another name? What name did Schaeffer know you by?"

"You don't seem to be making any sense," she said flatly. "That hit on the head you took—"

"I've got someone checking old NYU records and yearbooks," I told her. "Several people, in fact. They're undoubtedly on the job already. I told them to trace Joe Jenkins—Robert Joseph Janski—then look for you. How's that for sense?"

"Worse than ever. Listen, Matt, does Kenni know you're here?"

"As a matter of fact, Kenni doesn't. Several other people do, though. I didn't want to upset Kenni until it was all over. She likes you, you know. I liked you, too. I suppose you're good at that. You're very intelligent, maybe even brilliant. And I don't suppose you actually *hate* people, you just don't give a single flying shit about anybody but yourself."

"That's enough, Matt. Get out of here, right now." She pointed to the door, just in case I'd forgotten the way.

"When I've told you what I have to tell you."

She was angry. She stood up to her full five-one or so. "If you're not leaving, I am. And I'll be back with a policeman."

I said, "Spot, watch."

The Samoyed rose from a squat to a crouch. He pulled his smile back to show a mouthful of very white, very pointy teeth. He snarled a little, then made hungry sounds in the back of his throat.

"You can go to jail for this, damn you," she said.

"Nah. If this works one way, this is a citizen's arrest. If it works out the other way, it won't even matter that much. Sit down," I told her. "Relax. Nobody's going to hurt you. Certainly not me or Spot, unless you go for a gun or something."

She sat back down. "You won't get away with this," she said.

"That's my line," I said. "You know, the funny thing is, you *might* have gotten away with it. I was inclined to do this by the book, you know, send my people through the records, establish the connection between you and Janski, build a case for the authorities. I realized in that time you could clear out of here with the diamonds—you did get the diamonds, didn't you?"

"I don't," she said distinctly, "know what you're talking about."

"You got them," I said. "And you got them through Customs,

too. Nice touch. They weren't likely to suspect someone of smuggling who volunteered to spend a half hour filling out forms and paying duties. Especially since they'd no reason to be looking. Gardeno didn't tell them anything. I'm sure the diamonds are in the bank. They were safe in a bank on the Island for years, and American banks are just as safe, even if they do demand names."

I leaned back in my chair. "As I was saying, I knew if you took off you'd have the most portable form of vast wealth available to you, and that you'd probably take off before we were ready to do anything about you, but you could be chased, and eventually found, and my conscience would be clear.

"Until this afternoon, Jan. Until you shook my hand and smiled at me and told me how much you enjoyed the trip. You meant it. You've killed four men, Jan, and nearly killed two more people, one of whom was me. And you loved every minute of it. You thought you were tweaking me, laughing at me, at all us suckers, the way you'd been laughing at us all the whole trip. Maybe your whole life, for all I know.

"But you see, I'd already figured it out. You're shrewd and ruthless, and possibly brilliant, but you're not perfect. You made a few mistakes. You showed familiarity with the NYU community when you started talking about those saloons with Mike Ryerson. You left this"—I pulled the piece of plastic out of my pocket and showed it to her—"in Schaeffer's cabin. Missed it cleaning up, I suppose. No sin in that—the cabin steward missed it, too. You tried to kill me, which was a mistake in itself, and you failed to do it once you tried. That's when I figured it out, you see. Dangling over the ocean like a tea bag. People are supposed to see their lives flash before them at a time like that—I saw *your* life, at least your life since you decided to rip off the Mafia. What I didn't see clearly, I got a pretty good idea of—like how you arranged to win the contest, and why Janski was killed, and why Schaeffer and Burkehart got it, and where Schaeffer went to, and how I got a note from a dead man. The only thing I haven't been able to figure out is why you tortured Schaeffer before you killed him."

Jan looked hatred at me. The last time I had seen a look that hostile it had been on the face of Lee H. Schaeffer.

"It had to be that. You conked him on the head, got him tied to a chair or something, and burned him with his hair dryer. You broke the plastic nose off so that you could get the hot metal elements against his skin. I went round and round on this piece of plastic and that burn mark on the floor. It didn't mean anything to me at the time. Another bad break you got was that I am used to looking stupid, and I'm willing to do it if I have to. Nobody can say you didn't *try* to keep me away from Gardeno, and God knows you were angry enough when I went. Now I know why. Once I heard the M.O. of the torture murder of Gardeno's nephew, I might put the burn mark on the rug in perspective.

"All it meant was that you toasted Schaeffer's toes a little, right? Did you hate him that much, or were you trying to get something out of him?"

Jan's stare had lost some hatred. It was almost speculative now.

"The thing that gets me," I went on, "is that you were already planning to kill him. I don't know how you got Burkehart to steal the knives for you, but—and there I go again. Everyone keeps saying 'knives.' But it was more than a set of knives. It was a *full set of butcher's tools*. There are knives in there, sure. But there are also cleavers of various sizes, and a *bone saw*.

"Schaeffer was *always* headed out that porthole, wasn't he? But he was too big to fit *through* the porthole. So somehow, you arranged it so he could be made to fit. My guess is you sawed one arm off at the shoulder, washed blood down the drain until most of it was gone, wrapped the cut ends in the plastic from his dry cleaning, threw the arm out the porthole, and dragged the rest of the body across, pushed that out the porthole, and followed up with the knives and hair dryer. How am I doing so far?"

Jan ran her finger along her chin. "I wonder," she said, "what I would find if I searched *you* right now."

"Muscle and hair," I told her. "I'm not wearing a wire, if that's what you mean."

"Oh, I'll just bet you're not. Still, I don't think you're as smart as you think you are."

I grinned at her. "Care to tell me where I'm wrong?"

"Matt, dear, you're *wrong* from beginning to end. But even in the realm of your own fantasy, I think I could explain things better."

"Go right ahead," I suggested.

"This is only fantasy, you understand. Complete fantasy. Nothing like it ever happened, or ever could happen. But I think a really clever killer would have had *Schaeffer* arrange to have the cutlery stolen.''

"However would she do that?" I asked. I was beginning to regret that I *hadn't* arranged to wear a wire. When I'd come here this afternoon, I'd had two ends in mind—to satisfy as much of my own curiosity as possible, and to stall for time until various organizations could get their asses in gear. I knew Jan was a psychopath, but I didn't really expect her to be such a classic psychopath, the kind with the ego burning to have you know how *clever* they are, how they've been able to get away with things a mere human is frightened to think of. The kick of doing it wears off; the kick of having them *knowing* you did it lasts forever, because they're hemmed in by their silly rules, and all they can do is gnash their teeth, and curse you in their impotence. I remembered how angry she was when I said to come in before she knocked. She's the one who had to be making the mysteries.

As she was doing now. I was the promising student. I'd seen through to some of her glory. Now I was going to get a chance to appreciate the rest.

Because she knew she was safe. She knew where all the evidence was. Most was at the bottom of the ocean, the rest was hidden by her in places no one could open until she died. And she would never die. She was too smart to die.

I played my part. "How could she get Schaeffer to do that?" I asked.

"Oh, well, you can't just hypothesize in a vacuum, you know. It takes background. Oh, and by the way, you were right about one thing—"

"One whole thing?"

"I did go to NYU, you know, and I did take a class with Schaeffer. I didn't like him. That's why I pretended not to know him on the ship.''

"And that explains why he kept staring at you. So my people will find you somewhere in the old yearbooks and records."

"They might. I had a lot of puppy fat then. And I used a different name. Even if they did find me, it wouldn't prove anything, would it? I mean, Schaeffer may have stared, but he never actually recognized me. And I preferred not to remind him."

She grinned at me. She was beginning to enjoy this. "Of course, in the hypothesis, it's different."

"I'll just bet."

So she made me a hypothesis, about a young girl from upstate New York who comes to the Big City to live in Greenwich Village and go to college. And the young girl meets a young man and thinks she loves him, but succumbs instead to the charms of a professor. The young man gets into trouble and gets kicked out of school, and the professor soon gets tired of her, and dumps her. Just before finals, at which time he gives her a D.

The young woman takes the rejection badly—the young are such fools, don't you think? She drops out of school, breaks contact with her parents. Becomes an airline flight attendant. Sees a lot of the world. Grows up. Sees life for what it really is. Learns that men are *easy*. Hates herself for what she let the professor do to her.

"Don't you agree men are easy?" she said.

I told her I'd never thought about it.

"Well, think about it now," she said. "It's your theory I'm this terrible person. If that were true, which of course it's not, I managed you the whole trip, knew everything you were doing, without even having to lower myself enough to sleep with you. How much easier can you get?"

I smiled at her. "Go on with your hypothesis."

She went on. One day, the young man she had thought herself to be in love with turns up on one of her flights. They have dinner. He tells her he is into big money, and she could help him, if she wanted. She sees the young man now as a bastard in training, lacking only experience in rottenness to be just as bad as the professor had been, but she strings along because she is fascinated with the operation. She sees that the key to the whole thing is the number of that bank box on St. David's Island. She knows she can be ruthless enough to get it, and convinces the young man he can be, too.

She does the work while the young man stands there and cringes, but they get the number. But something goes wrong. They plan to get the—

"What was it you said, diamonds?"

"Don't be too coy, Jan. I said diamonds back on the ship."

—to get the diamonds when the Mafia boss goes to jail, but he doesn't go to jail. He sits, figuratively, on the doorstep of the bank, waiting for them to return. She could go and get the diamonds herself, but Janski calls her every night. He doesn't trust her. He's told her that if she's ever not home, he will tell Gardeno who she is and the best places to find her.

Stalemate. But things aren't so bad. They can still raise half a million or so from the dope they haven't delivered. So they do. This is split fairly amicably. The young woman opens a shop. The young man goes into radio, eventually working his way back to New York.

But the diamonds sit there, on the island, winking in the darkness of the vault, mocking them. It's frustrating, maddening.

Then they get a break. The radio station the young man works for decides on a contest to send someone to St. David's Island. The young man arranges that he'll go with the winner.

"And then," I said, "he arranges for you to be the winner."

"Me?" she said in mock horror. "Matt, this is only a hypothesis."

"Sure it is," I said agreeably. "I just like to use people's names instead of 'the young man,' or 'the young woman.'"

"It's simple," I went on. "Instead of a random phone call, he calls you. The real genius is the use of Kenni as a beard. It's a mystery quiz, you have an acquaintance who's a mystery nut, and you arrange for her to provide you with the answers. I remember being told about the 'wrong number' you got just before the contest came in. That was Janski checking to make sure Kenni was there.

"And while I'm hypothesizing, I might as well add that I should have been on to you sooner."

Jan was in absolute heaven by now. I was good enough at this to make an enjoyable game of it, but there was no way I could touch her. She thought.

"Oh?" she said. "Why is that?"

"Because you're *short*. You're strong, but you're short. When you think about it, swinging *up* at the back of someone's head is an inefficient way to cool him. That's why you got into the habit of flattening heads afterwards, or of shoving people overboard after you'd stunned them. You simply couldn't reach high enough to make sure of putting a man out with one shot. You made up for it with persistence."

"Interesting point," she said. There was a hint of a grin on her lips. "May I go on?"

I nodded, and she talked some more. Assume, she said, that my hypothesizing was correct (and she congratulated me for having an imagination that fit in so well with hers) what happened next?

She could imagine, she said, the young woman, once her passage had been assured, getting rid of the weak and potentially treacherous young man once and for all, and preparing for the trip. She was unknown—it would be a simple matter for her to elude her guest and her Network companion long enough to hit the bank and retrieve the diamonds.

But just before it's time to leave, she learns the professor, now a writer, will be on the trip. The man who had seduced and abandoned her in her innocent youth. A man who knew she'd been acquainted with Janski.

She considers canceling out on the trip, but she's waited so long, and done so much work. She hates to think she killed Janski and lugged his loathsome carcass through Riverside Park in the dead of night for *nothing*. Besides, she will likely never have another chance as good as this.

So she decides to risk it. The ship is fairly large; perhaps she can avoid Schaeffer. She didn't realize how clubby these game-players would be—that they would eat together, be together all the time. She didn't reckon on the efficiency of Network Publicity, who threw them together before the ship even left port.

She doesn't really look the same, but sometime during that first day, Schaeffer recognizes her. Secretly, after the boat drill, he passes her a note.

"Signed 'Lee,'" I said. "Only women he slept with called him Lee."

"We must hypothesize together more often," she said.

So Lee will have to be dealt with. She keeps the note, in case it might cone in handy for future mystification. Then she turns her attention to Lee. Men are easy, especially men with egos the size of Lee's. Lee has developed a feud with the Network representative, a young man he hates at first sight. The young woman meets with Lee in secret later that afternoon, and tells him she will be his spy in the enemy camp. She'll have to pretend to hate him Lee grins, says he understands. She can slap his face if she wants to Just help him show this Cobb his place.

Jan says of course, but she has another idea. Lee has mentioned that he's retained the Acting Chief Dining Room Steward to harass you at mealtime. The young woman suggests that he bribe the man to steal some serious cutlery from the galley. When Lee asks why, she tells him it will be a surprise. Her surprises in the old days had always been worthwhile, and so he agrees.

Late that night, she sneaks to his cabin. This is ostensibly to be a sympathy screw for his having lost the Ping-Pong game, but Jan has other games in mind.

It is essential that she know whether Lee has told anyone on or off the ship about her. She had been the man's lover; she knows denials from him are worthless—he'll tell her what he thinks she ought to hear, which rarely has any relation to the truth.

So she gets behind him and hits him with his complimentary bottle of champagne. She strips him and ties him up, and is about to drag him to the bathroom and put the knives to work as truth insurance, when she sees the hair dryer and decides that will be much easier, less messy. She breaks off the protective plastic nose by closing the porthole on it She plugs the dryer in, lets it get hot, and waits for Lee to regain consciousness.

Lee's cabin is directly below the disco—chances are no screams would be heard. Still, she takes no chances, gagging him while she applies the hot metal to his flesh, removing the gag to let him make his whimpered denials. The rug gets a little scorched, so she leaves his feet alone after that.

She takes her time, does a thorough job. She knows her roommate plans to be occupied in the bed of the triumphant Ping-Pong warrior. The stars in her eyes and lust in her loins will keep her busy well past dawn.

When she is quite sure Lee has told no one, she picks up the champagne bottle and finishes the job. She tries to throw him overboard, but makes a distressing discovery—his shoulders are too wide to fit through the porthole. Or maybe she's planned it this way all along. The bathroom and the butcher's tools become useful after all Lee (wrapped in plastic), the cutlery, and the hair dryer all go out the porthole, where the Atlantic will keep her secrets. The champagne bottle, wiped of fingerprints, goes back in the bucket.

After that, she has an amusing couple of days feigning seasickness, as everyone, especially this oh-so-impressive young man from the Network, tries to figure out what's happened to Lee.

But then the young man goes to work on Burkehart, and Burkehart has promised to tell him "everything." Chances are, "everything" is simply that he stole the knives for the missing Mr. Schaeffer. These people liked games; the young woman was obliging them by leading them in a game. And it would have been an amusing play to let Burkehart talk, if that were all he really had to say.

Unfortunately, she couldn't take that chance. She had to isolate Burkehart, then dispose of him; to do that, she had to confront him. Once she'd done that, there was no *choice* but to kill him.

She takes a chance. She gets a message to him, and meets him on deck late at night. She could kill him right there, but the night is too nice—someone might take a walk on deck and see them together. She decides to wait. She gives him a thousand dollars to jump ship outside the harbor, promising more when they meet on the island next day. Burkehart tells her about the isolated beach.

The poisoned coffee has already assured that she'll be alone to keep the rendezvous. Which she does. On the way back to the ship, wearing a blond wig, she stops at the bank and gets the diamonds.

She should be home free. She *is* home free. No one can convict her, no one can *touch* her.

But the young woman wants more than that. She doesn't want to be *bothered*. She has worked hard for the money, and she wants to be left to spend it in peace. And then, the night of the tropical storm, the young man from the Network talks of digging up the past. He will find the young woman's connection with Janski and with Schaeffer. She doesn't want that to happen; she doesn't want him to get back to New York and start that process in motion. She'll take care of him somehow. Men are easy.

She isn't seasick, she never is. Her roommate has taken Dramamine, and is asleep. The young woman can always say she went out for air—no one suspects her, no one ever will. She watches the Network man's cabin, trying to think of a way to get him to let her inside. He *might* fit through the porthole, but there's the dog to deal with. The dog likes her, but will he stand still while she kills his master? Can she kill the dog without getting herself marked up?

The problem solves itself when the cabin door opens, and a seasick young man lurches upstairs and out on deck. She has armed herself with her own champagne bottle. There will be no casual strollers on deck tonight. She follows him, unseen, and attacks. It doesn't quite go according to plan, though. *She* almost winds up over the rail. She runs away while her man is still dazed and wiping rain from his eyes. Maybe the wind will sweep him over the side. She's back in her cabin and under the shower in five minutes. This is both to calm her, and to explain to her roommate, should she awaken, why she's wet. But the matter never comes up. The roommate sleeps like the dead; too much sex, lately, the young woman supposes.

The next day they reach New York. The diamonds are stowed safely away. The young man from the Network may make a nuisance of himself, but there is nothing he can do.

"Is there?" Jan said, smiling sweetly.

"Is there what?"

"If our hypothesis were true, instead of the pure fantasy it is, there isn't a single thing you could do about it, could you?"

"Sure there is," I said. "I could torture you and make you tell me where the diamonds are."

"All that would get you is a prison term. You'd need me to get the diamonds, and you wouldn't dare trust me out of your sight. Just as Janski wouldn't. Besides, even if by some miracle you could get these"—she smiled—"*hypothetical* diamonds, you wouldn't. Why, Kenni tells me even Martin Gardeno spotted you for an honest man."

"No," I said. "You're right. I wouldn't do that."

"Then will you please let me get to work? I'm very tired of your mystery games, Mr. Cobb." She stood up. Spot sprang to his feet and barked and snarled and showed his teeth. Jan turned white and backed against the wall.

I permitted myself a small smile. "Back, Spot, back," I said. Spot turned into a friendly house pet again. I looked at my watch. "Yes, I guess I'd better go. Kenni is waiting for me."

Jan gave me the smuggest smile yet. "I'm sure you'll be very good for each other. Come on, I'll let you out."

We went back into the shop. As we crossed the floor, Jan said, "You know, Matt, if that resourceful young woman we fantasized about really existed, you would have offended her terribly. She'd probably want revenge. You'd have to be very careful never to offend her again."

I looked out the shop window to Columbus Avenue.

"Oh, good," I said. "One of them's here."

Jan unlocked the door. "One of what?" she said.

"Well," I said. "Let *me* hypothesize for a while. Suppose a different young man met a young woman—a vicious, conscienceless psychopath who had committed crimes the law could never touch her for, unless she confessed and led them to the evidence herself. And suppose the young man had been part of her plan, unwittingly. And let's further hypothesize that while the young man is honest, and a good-natured enough sort, he grew up on the streets of New York— where he acquired a code that never left him. Mess with me, and regret it. What would he do?"

Jan shrugged prettily. "Come to the young woman? Try his caveman act? Maybe bring along an animal with teeth in an attempt to scare her?"

I looked out the window. "Oh. There's another one."

"Another *what*?" she demanded. There was anger in her voice.

"Another big black sedan. The one closest to the door will probably have first crack." I turned to Jan. "Caveman act? Nah. If he did that at all, it would merely be to kill time until the real plan took effect.

"You see, what he would do would be to make a few phone calls. One would be to the Drug Enforcement Agency officer back on the island. Another would be to Inspector Buxton, of the Royal St. David's Island Constabulary, who would ask the NYPD to send an unmarked car and hold the suspect until he could arrive in New York and question her."

Jan's eyes were wide. I gave her my biggest smile. "And the third call—"

"You wouldn't."

"Mess with me, and regret it," I said cheerfully. "The third would go to the man whose beloved nephew you tortured to death. The man who has astonished his doctors by living on, inspired solely by the desire to get his hands on you. Even before he knew who you were."

"But—but—"

"I called him last," I said. "That's more consideration than you deserve."

"It's . . . it's *murder*. You wouldn't dare!"

"What's the matter? You the only one who gets to murder people? You've got a better chance than you gave anyone else. Besides, you're too dangerous to let run around loose."

I grabbed the door handle. "The deal was, as soon as I leave, the people outside can move in. So let's hypothesize about what happens next. If they're both from the Mafia, you've had it."

Jan's head was shaking involuntarily from side to side, no, no, no.

"I don't think they will be. Gardeno's organization is efficient, but I told him the cops had a head start. If it's Mafia people out there, they're just to watch.

"So if it's cops, you go and talk to them. Buxton tells me the penalty for murder is only twenty-five years on St. David's Island. You can work on your tan, maybe as you harvest guano for the fertilizer plant, I don't know. Or you can talk to the DEA and go to a federal women's prison. You should be reasonably safe—I don't know that I've ever heard of the Mafia ordering a hit inside a women's prison. Of course, there's always a first time.

"Of course, as we've said over and over, only you can provide the proof to convict you. If you tough it out, the cops will have to let you go.

"And Gardeno's people will be waiting. How do you like the game now, Jan?"

She kept staring at me in disbelief. Psychopaths believe that they alone are exempt from the rules. It offends them deeply when someone else puts a dent in what they consider proper.

"Of course, there's one more possibility. You lied to me, and there is another way out of here, or you manage to hop out of the police or DEA car on the way downtown, or you convince them to let you go before Gardeno's New York people can cover you.

"In a way, I like that one the best. The banks are closed now—no diamonds. You wouldn't dare go home. You wouldn't dare come back here. You'd have to split, today, now, with the clothes on your back and the money in your pocket—the cops will take away your purse—and elude the Mafia the rest of your life. It would be just like before. Except now Gardeno will know who you are and what you look like. And federal and New York cops would be after you, too."

I turned the knob. "Good-bye, Jan. Maybe you can charm your way out of this. Men are easy. Meeting you has been a real experience." I opened the door.

She grabbed the front of my shirt. "You *can't!*" she screamed.

Gently, I disengaged fingers from cloth. "I did," I said softly. "Pleasant dreams."

I let Spot out, then followed him. Somebody in a black car tapped on a horn. I waved and nodded to a shape behind a tinted windshield.

Kenni was waiting. I didn't even hang around to see who got out of the car.